"I told you I never stay in one place for long."

It was a well-honed protective mechanism. Never get too attached—to people or places—because it's so much easier to cope when they're not there any longer. "A year or two and I'll be moving on again. That's the way I roll. As I said, I like you, Jo, and age is just a number. It doesn't make the slightest difference. Not to me." He held her gaze. "But maybe it does for you? If you're looking for something more…significant?"

She shook her head. "I think I gave up on the idea of significant a long time ago. I've had too many dead-end relationships. I've watched too many other marriages disintegrate, including my brothers'. I do have another confession, though."

"What's that?" There was a sparkle in her eyes now that he'd seen somewhere before. Oh, no…she wasn't about to tell him that she was falling in love with him, was she?

She took a deep breath. "I'm planning to have a baby," she said.

Dear Reader,

I've got a meme that has resonated on so many levels for me. It's a picture of two white circles on a dark background. There's an arrow pointing to the center of the small circle labeled "Your Comfort Zone." Inside the big circle are the words *Where the Magic Happens*.

In any aspect of life, I find it can be all too easy to stay in that comfort zone, but the inspiration of this image to push myself in new directions in the hope of finding magic has yet to wear off, and that applies to my storytelling along with other things like new travel destinations or meeting new people or just trying an unfamiliar cuisine.

Jo, my heroine in *A Paramedic to Change Her Life*, has decided to make a huge leap out of one of her own comfort zones and she's hoping for the magic of being able to become a mother before it's too late. There's another comfort zone she might also need to step out of—if she wants to keep the extra magic she's found—but I'll leave that one for you to discover.

Happy reading!

With love,

Alison xx

A PARAMEDIC
TO CHANGE HER LIFE

ALISON ROBERTS

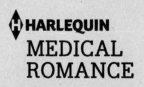

HARLEQUIN

MEDICAL
ROMANCE

HARLEQUIN®
MEDICAL
ROMANCE™

Recycling programs
for this product may
not exist in your area.

ISBN-13: 978-1-335-73722-9

A Paramedic to Change Her Life

Copyright © 2022 by Alison Roberts

For questions and comments about the quality of this book, please contact us at CustomerService@Harlequin.com.

Harlequin Enterprises ULC
22 Adelaide St. West, 41st Floor
Toronto, Ontario M5H 4E3, Canada
www.Harlequin.com

Printed in U.S.A.

Alison Roberts has been lucky enough to live in the south of France for several years recently but is now back in her home country of New Zealand. She is also lucky enough to write for the Harlequin Medical Romance line. A primary school teacher in a former life, she later became a qualified paramedic. She loves to travel and dance, drink champagne, and spend time with her daughter and her friends. Alison Roberts is the author of over one hundred books!

Books by Alison Roberts

Harlequin Medical Romance

Two Tails Animal Refuge

The Vet's Unexpected Family

Twins Reunited on the Children's Ward

A Pup to Rescue Their Hearts
A Surgeon with a Secret

Royal Christmas at Seattle General

Falling for the Secret Prince

Unlocking the Rebel's Heart
Stolen Nights with the Single Dad
Christmas Miracle at the Castle
Miracle Baby, Miracle Family

Visit the Author Profile page
at Harlequin.com for more titles.

CHAPTER ONE

THE FIRST CLUE that it might be harder than usual for Dr Joanna Bishop to ignore the significance of this particular day of the year came in the form of the rather startling noise of a nearby car horn.

Not that she had any premonition of the ripple effect the noise might have, of course. All she was thinking about, as she looked through the glass doors of the exterior entrance, was why someone might have parked a car at such an odd angle in the ambulance bay of Dunedin's Princess Margaret Hospital's emergency department and why they were now leaning repeatedly on the horn. Clearly, assistance was needed. Urgently.

Pulling on gloves as she moved swiftly to follow a triage nurse and registrar through the double sets of sliding doors, she could see frantic movement around the car as the driver jumped out and opened a back door.

A security guard was opening the other door. By the time Jo reached the car, the male driver was halfway into the back seat on the driver's side. A woman had one leg out of the vehicle on the other side but was clinging to the sides of the passenger seat in front of her. And screaming.

'Oh, my God…the baby's coming… Like, right *now*…'

'She started having contractions all of a sudden.' The man sounded terrified. 'About twenty minutes ago. I didn't think we were going to make it. I didn't know what to do…'

'You've done exactly the right thing,' Jo told him. She tucked the front locks of her short, dark bob behind her ears, bent down to the woman, who was still lost in her pain, and put one hand on her back to let her know she wasn't alone. She put her other hand on what looked to be a belly in the late stages of pregnancy to feel the iron-hard clench of contracting muscles. They couldn't try moving her from the car just yet but they would need to be ready when the contraction ended because an upward glance revealed clouds that looked threatening enough to be about to resume the heavy rain showers they'd been having on and off all morning.

Jo turned to the senior triage nurse beside her but she didn't need to say anything.

'I'll grab a wheelchair,' Hanna said. 'And an obstetrics kit—just in case.'

Jo nodded her approval of Hanna's initiative. She needed to raise her voice to talk to the woman's partner over the sound of the loud groaning. 'How often are the contractions happening?'

'I dunno. Every couple of minutes?' The man wriggled further onto the back seat and sounded as if he was on the verge of tears now. 'It's not supposed to be happening like this.'

'How many weeks along is she?'

'Thirty-six.'

'Just the one baby?'

'Yeah.'

'Have there been any problems with the pregnancy?'

'No.' The man's face twisted. 'Not until now...' He put his arm around his wife's shoulders. 'It's okay, babe. We're here now. You're gonna be okay...'

He seemed to be trying to reassure himself as much as the woman, but for Jo there was relief to be found in knowing that this was a singleton pregnancy that was this close to full term. A high-risk situation like a very premature delivery or the imminent arrival of twins or triplets would have rung much louder alarm bells, but Jo still turned to the young doctor beside her.

'Page whoever's on call from Obstetrics, please, David. And let's get someone from Paediatrics down as well.' If this was going to turn into the fairly rare event of a birth in the emergency department Jo still needed to plan for any complications such as post-partum haemorrhage for the mother or a newborn with a respiratory arrest. They had two patients here.

It was also a relief to feel the rigidity beneath her hand beginning to soften. The woman's contraction, along with her groaning, was beginning to subside.

'I'm Jo,' she introduced herself, 'one of the doctors here. We're going to take good care of you and your baby. What's your name?'

'She's Susie,' her partner answered for her. 'She's my wife.'

'Is this your first baby?'

'Yeah…'

Still clinging to the passenger seat, Susie's breath came out in a sob. 'I think I'm bleeding. There's something horribly wrong, isn't there?' She turned her head to hide her face against her partner. 'Jack… I'm *scared*…'

Jack put both arms around her. They were both crying.

'You're not bleeding.' Jo had already checked what she could see of the towel Susie was sitting on. 'You're feeling wet because your waters have broken, which is perfectly normal at this stage of labour.' There was some staining in the fluid that could be meconium, which would suggest the baby was stressed, but Susie didn't need to know that. 'Let's get you inside before your next contraction and then we'll be able to see what's happening.'

Hanna was beside her again, with a wheelchair that she was using to carry a blanket, the equipment roll that contained things that might be needed for a birth, like clamps, scissors and a scalpel, pads and a suction bulb. She had also thought to grab a cylinder of Entonox but it quickly became apparent that providing Susie with inhaled pain relief, let alone trying to move her into a more desirable environment might not be possible. She was gasping, crying out and trying to speak all at the same time.

'It's coming... I can feel the head... Oh... *Oh...*'

There was a short period of controlled chaos as Susie was helped to turn onto her back, her upper body cradled against her husband as she lay on the back seat of the car and staff rushed to respond to orders for supplies like oxygen, an IV trolley and towels and to find out whether the specialist consults had arrived in the department yet.

Hanna used shears from the obstetrics kit she had unrolled to cut through clothing and they could both see that Susie was quite right—her baby's head was visible and about to be born. Jo's priority, as she knelt beside the car, was to try and control the speed with which it happened, by putting gentle pressure on the baby's head, to minimise trauma to both mother and baby.

As soon as the head had emerged, Jo used her finger to check for the position of the umbilical cord and found it around the baby's neck. Her careful attempt to bring it over the baby's head or even loosen it was unsuccessful.

'It's too tight,' she told Hanna. 'I'll have to clamp and cut it.'

Hanna handed her two clamps and then the sterile scissors to cut through the cord between them. Delivery of the baby had just become more urgent but, although Jo could feel that Susie was pushing, there was no progress to be seen in the movement of the baby's body.

'We're nearly there, Susie. Give me a really big push.'

Jo kept her voice calm but Hanna had picked up on the urgency as she held onto Susie's legs to support her.

'You're doing so well,' she told the young mother. 'One more big push, hon. Hard as you can. Push, push, *push*...'

In her peripheral vision, Jo caught the arrival of the obstetric consultant but there was no way she could hand over the management of this birth at this critical moment. She was holding the baby with both hands and she pushed gently downwards to free the first shoulder and then applied upward traction to free the second. The rest of the baby boy's body slid out rapidly and, at the same time, there was a loud, warbling cry from the infant that sparked an audible sigh of relief from the group of medical staff surrounding Jo and Hanna, a nod of approval from the obstetrician and the sight of both the first-time parents bursting into tears.

The baby was moving and clearly breathing well enough to cry so the priority was to keep him warm and get both mother and baby into the emergency department for a thorough assessment and the next Apgar score, which was due at five minutes after birth. Hanna handed Jo a warm, dry towel which she used to wrap around the infant, cradling him in her arms, and she got to her feet so that she could hand the baby to his mother as soon as she'd been helped into the wheelchair.

It had been a very long time since Jo had delivered a baby and, on that occasion, it had been put straight onto the mother's abdomen so it was even longer since she'd held one in her own arms. For just a heartbeat she looked down at the crumpled, angry little face of this tiny human that had just entered the world rather abruptly and it felt... heartbreaking.

Not in a bad way. It felt as if something had broken that had been filled with a liquid warmth that was now seeping, with the speed of light, right through Jo's body. The kind of warmth that came from the best of what life could ever offer. The kind of warmth that only really came from human connection.

From love...

Susie was in the wheelchair now, blankets around her shoulders and tears streaming down her face as she held her arms out for her baby.

'Here you go. He's just gorgeous.' Jo carefully transferred the bundle and had to blink away a tear or two of her own. 'This little guy's had a birthday you're never going to forget, hasn't he?'

She stayed where she was for a moment, peeling off her gloves, as Susie was wheeled into the department. She could see that her colleagues from both the obstetric and paediatric departments had already taken over the care of mother and baby so her own part in this drama was no longer essential and, well… Jo needed to take a quick breath before joining them to continue any involvement in the case.

Hanna rolled up the sterile cloth that had contained the scissors and clamps.

'Reckon this is one you're never going to forget either.' Her smile widened. 'Happy Birthday, Jo.'

Jo couldn't smile back at her friend. If anything, she could feel her expression becoming quite sombre. It wasn't because she didn't want to think about her own birthday—she was looking forward to the planned celebration with Hanna after work, where they were going to try the tapas and sangria at the new Spanish restaurant in town.

No. It was because something much more important was happening. Jo could still feel that odd warmth that holding the baby had triggered and it felt as if a switch had been flicked, in her head as well as her heart.

'You know what?'

'What?' Hanna's eyebrows rose and then lowered into a concerned frown. 'Are you okay, Jo?'

'Never better.' Jo led the way back into the emergency department. 'I've just realised something.'

'Oh?'

Jo pulled in a deep breath as she turned her head. 'If I don't do it now, I never will because it'll be too late. It might be too late already but I won't know until I try, will I?'

'Oh, no…' Hanna stopped in her tracks before the automatic door could be triggered ahead of them. 'Delivering that baby has blown a fuse, hasn't it? You want one of your own?'

'I've always wanted one. One day. It's just never been the right time. And it never will be if I keep waiting for it to arrive. It's my birthday, Hanna. I'm forty-six.' Jo blew out a breath. How on earth had that apparently sneaked up on her? 'Forty. *Six*. Time isn't just running out…it's disappearing around the corner.'

'But…'

Was Hanna about to point out that Jo didn't even have a man in her life, let alone a partner to raise a child with? Jo didn't need to be reminded. It was also time to stop this snatched conversation and get back to work, but Hanna was looking worried now. As if she thought Jo might be completely losing the plot?

'There's something you don't know about me,' Jo told her. 'Something nobody knows.'

'Go on then… Tell me. I can keep a secret.'

But Jo shook her head. 'We can't talk about it here.'

'Just as well we're going out for dinner then, isn't it?' Hanna followed her inside.

Jo was already switching off from anything personal as she walked towards the resuscitation area that Susie and her baby had been taken to. She'd have to tell Hanna about it later because she'd already opened the bag that contained the cat, hadn't she? And when she started talking about it out loud it would become real and would end up changing her life.

But that was okay. Because that feeling was only getting stronger and it ramped up to a new level as she walked into Resus and saw Susie cradling her baby boy on the bed beside her.

The fuse *had* blown. The switch *had* been flicked. And Jo *had* meant what she'd said.

It really was now or never.

'*Whoa.*'

'It's all good, mate.' Cade Cameron threw the briefest of glances towards his junior crew partner, who was reaching to catch the water bottle that was sliding off his lap. 'I know what I'm doing.'

But his partner, Geoff, was grinning. 'I know. Word is that you've done a bit of rally car racing back in the day.'

Cade didn't look sideways again as the next twist of the hilly road demanded his full focus. 'Yeah…it's been one of my hobbies in the past. Off road driving too.'

Flickers of colour from the flashing beacons on the roof of the vehicle were lighting up the shadows of the pine forest they were driving through and reflecting on the wet tarmac beneath them. There wasn't much traffic on this road now that they were well out of the city so Cade didn't flick the siren again until they were behind a logging truck that obligingly slowed and pulled to the left as they reached a straighter stretch. Cade put his foot down then.

This was great. His first day in his new job and he was getting one of his favourite kinds of callout. Outdoors. Away from any main roads. Something that could well provide the kind of challenge an adrenaline junkie thrived on. Even the weather looked as if it was going to add another level to an unknown and potentially dangerous situation and that was fine by Cade.

Bring it on...

'Any more info coming through?'

Geoff scrolled through the information on screen. 'Twenty-three-year-old female. Slipped and fell while crossing a creek. Her leg's wedged between boulders up to her knee and she was in too much pain when they made an attempt to pull her free. They were worried that the leg could be fractured and they might be making things worse. She's conscious and cold.'

Cade was checking another screen that was providing his GPS, noting that he needed to slow down so that he didn't miss the upcoming turnoff. His thoughts, however, were mostly with a young woman who was in severe pain, possible losing blood and almost certainly very frightened. The sooner they got there, the better. It had already taken too long to get here from the central city.

'Who's on scene already?'

'There were three others on the tramp, all uni students. Two forestry guys who were working nearby heard someone yelling for help. They happen to be part of the local search and rescue team, knew that mobile phone reception can be dodgy out here and they texted someone who called emergency services. One of them will be waiting for us at the car park to show us the way and help carry any gear. It's about a fifteen to twenty-minute walk uphill to the scene. Fire service and police are on the way. ETA another five to ten minutes. Sounds like we might need their heavy gear and more manpower to shift a rock or two.'

Cade nodded. 'We'll see what we can do before they get here as long as it's safe for everybody. Might be a good workout for us. Any update on air rescue? We'll be well over forty minutes from the hospital if we factor in getting down that track.'

'They're still transporting a patient to hospital. Could be a while before they're clear.'

Cade turned into the parking area, making a mental note that it was big enough for a helicopter to land as long as the fire trucks and police vehicles stayed on the road. He also noted the steep set of wooden stairs that marked the start of the forest track. Shifting rocks wasn't the only workout they had ahead of them, with at least a fifteen-minute walk to reach the scene and having to carry a lot of gear, including a scoop stretcher, trauma pack, oxygen tank and life pack. There were fat raindrops hitting the windscreen as they came to a halt and he could see the grim expressions on the faces of the two men who were waiting for them.

'We know this area,' one of them told Cade as they prepared to set off up the track only a minute or two later, carrying a basket stretcher laden with gear. 'The girl's sitting in a creek that looks like nothing much but the water level can rise surprisingly fast with even a small amount of rain.' He turned up the collar of his raincoat. 'And this isn't a small amount.'

So Cade could add in a ticking clock to his assessment of environmental hazards before he even got to the scene. Yep…this was looking like a good challenge already. The urgency with which he got to the scene and gathered all the information he needed to determine just how serious this situation was—with both the condition of his patient and the environmental danger—made it feel as if time had sped up. Waiting for the air rescue helicopter to arrive, with the requested medical practitioner whose advanced skills he feared might be necessary if the only way to free this victim was by amputation of her trapped leg, made it feel as if time was going far too slowly.

And then, when the helicopter crew arrived on scene at the creek, for just an instant, it felt as if time completely stopped.

It wasn't that the emergency specialist he'd requested was a woman that surprised him so much. Or that she'd made it up that steep track so fast that she had to be easily as fit as he was. No…it was more that he'd never seen a face that was so instantly captivating. Intelligent. Passionate.

Quite possibly the most intriguing face Cade had ever laid eyes on.

Not that she was looking at him as she got closer, mind you. Her focus, as it should be, was on the young woman he was holding in his arms to keep her head well away from the rising water of this creek—a task that was becoming progressively more difficult as the force of the water behind him steadily increased. But then her gaze flicked up and Cade got the full effect of having that focus on *him* and, crikey…he could swear it felt like some sort of electrical shock.

'I'm Jo Bishop,' she told him. 'Trauma specialist. Talk to me…'

CHAPTER TWO

THE SOUND OF water rushing over rocks could well turn out to be a trigger that would raise Joanna Bishop's adrenaline levels for the rest of her life but, right now, it was no more than a background noise that had to be ignored in order to gather essential information. Like whether this young woman had been knocked unconscious when she fell, if any other visible or suspected injuries had been noted and if her vital signs had deteriorated during the time it had taken for the helicopter crew to arrive on scene.

'Blood pressure's dropping.' The paramedic confirmed the worry that the patient's condition was getting less stable. 'Systolic was under a hundred last time we were able to record it. Her radial pulse isn't palpable now.'

Which meant that her blood pressure was

low enough to be dangerous. They needed to move fast. 'Blood loss?'

'Unknown. But she couldn't have been at the angle she was to her leg if it's not a major fracture so it's quite possibly compound. The water made it impossible to see if she's still bleeding.'

It did, because it was a huge volume of water and it was moving fast. The paramedic supporting this girl was a large man and his body was acting as an obstacle for water that was rushing past, in a wave that morphed into white foam as it coursed over the boulders downstream. Jo was grateful for the harness she was wearing and the fire officer who was holding the attached cable behind her in case the current made her lose her footing. Just behind them, the air rescue paramedics she had flown with were waiting for a signal to join her but, even though Jo had never met the man holding their patient, he was obviously going to be the person she needed to work with most closely. It would have been dangerous for the victim to try replacing him and Jo had the impression that he would have refused to move anyway. There was something very protective about his body language.

'I put a CAT on in case she was losing

blood from an open fracture or laceration but she's becoming hypothermic, which could well be contributing to the decrease in blood pressure.'

It was a wonder that the paramedic wasn't hypothermic himself. It might have finally stopped raining so heavily but Jo was already aware of how cold her feet were from just a short time being immersed in this swiftly flowing water. This man had been here for a much longer time but he wasn't even wearing his heavy duty emergency services' raincoat because it was wrapped around the patient he was holding and his arms were bare beneath the short sleeves of his uniform shirt.

A part of Jo's brain noted the edge of an inked pattern below the hem of a sleeve in passing and added it to information her brain was automatically gathering because it was in assessment mode, but the tattoo, along with this man's dark olive skin and the black curls of hair currently plastered to his skull, were instantly filed into an irrelevant category.

'How long since you put the tourniquet on?'

'Thirty-three minutes.'

The watch on the man's wrist looked like

something an elite soldier might wear and as if it could do a lot more than merely tell time, but it was helpful to know there was no need to think about loosening the Combat Application Tourniquet around the girl's thigh any time soon. Possibly not until they got her to hospital and even into Theatre. Jo could replace this item of the paramedic's gear with the same brand of tourniquet she had in the customised pouch in her own kit that was set up for amputation. The means of controlling both arterial and venous blood loss was tucked in amongst the scalpels and other surgical instruments like the Gigli saw—a flexible, serrated wire between two handles—that could be the best, perhaps only, device capable of a clean, precise cut through bone in a less than accessible space.

And maybe she didn't need the skills she knew her flight medic colleague could offer her by being the closest extra medic to this patient. She knew exactly how difficult it must have been to get an intravenous line in under these conditions, but there was a secure cannula in their patient's arm and someone in the knot of rescue workers nearby was holding up a bag of IV fluid.

'Good job getting the IV access before she was too shut down.' She caught his gaze again briefly to make sure he knew that she was impressed and not being patronising in any way. 'How much fluid has she had?'

'This is the second litre of saline. She's also had ten milligrams of morphine with good effect on pain levels.'

'GCS?'

'It was fifteen on arrival. She's responsive to voice but wasn't so oriented to time and place a few minutes ago.' He bent his head. 'Kayla? Open your eyes, sweetheart?'

Dark lashes, on a worryingly pale face, fluttered open and Jo could barely hear her voice. 'Where am I?'

'Still in the creek,' he told her. 'But we're going to get you out now. The cavalry's arrived.'

'But… I'm stuck…'

'We're going to unstick you.'

'How…?' The query was cut off as water suddenly surged under the paramedic's arm and washed right over Kayla's face. She coughed, choked and then cried out in pain as he tried to lift her a little higher, which must have put pressure on her leg.

'*No*… Oh…that *hurts*…'

Jo signalled to the helicopter crew that she needed her kit. Or, more precisely, the amputation pouch. Stat. Even in the few minutes she'd been standing in this creek the water level had risen noticeably. They needed to get more sedation on board for Kayla and get her out. Before she drowned. And, right now, it looked as if the only way they were going to achieve that was to do an above knee amputation.

Kayla was sobbing and her voice got loud enough to be very easy to hear. 'I don't want to die... Cade?'

'I'm here, darling.'

'Don't let me die... *Please* don't let me die...'

'I won't.'

'Promise...?'

'I promise.'

Uh-oh... Catching the surprised, swift glance of the trauma specialist made Cade realise that maybe he shouldn't have said that with such conviction. But it wasn't as though he hadn't meant it. He *wasn't* about to let Kayla die. Not if there was any way at all in the world he could prevent it, anyway.

And that meant staying right where he was, trying to protect Kayla from the full force of the creek's current and keeping her airway open as she was given enough seda-tion to lose consciousness and go limp in his arms. He was the only person in a position to monitor whether she was still breathing or had a pulse and, if either of those vital functions were lost, they'd have to get her somewhere they could try and resuscitate her in a matter of seconds.

'This won't take long.' There was a grim note in the doctor's voice and Cade could see that this woman was steeling herself to do something that went totally against her instincts. If she had the choice, she would be doing whatever she could to save the limb of this otherwise healthy young woman, not to be disabling her for the rest of her life by removing it. He could see the way she was gathering her courage as she picked up the scalpel after pouring disinfectant on bare skin. She would do this, and probably do it exceptionally well, if that was what it was going to take to save Kayla's life, but it was going to haunt her, wasn't it?

It would haunt everybody here.

'Wait…'

The glance he received this time was shocked.

'Let's give it one more try to shift this rock and pull her out.'

'*What?*' There was a flash of something like anger in that intense gaze. 'You mean you haven't tried everything you could already?'

'Of course we did. But…' Cade sucked in a breath. Was he about to anger this woman further by wasting time? It wasn't just loss of blood or the rising water that was putting Kayla in danger. She was getting progressively more hypothermic as well.

'*But…?*' The emphasis wasn't aggressive. She wanted to know what he had to say. Maybe she was hoping for a reprieve from having to go ahead with such a challenging procedure.

'I can feel the way her muscle tone's changed with the level of sedation she's under now.' Cade's words fell out rapidly. 'Maybe that could make a difference? What's the worst that can happen if there is a displaced fracture or partial amputation and we make it worse by dragging her out? She might lose her leg, but that's going to happen anyway, isn't it?'

She processed what he was saying in no more than a split second and then she turned and put the scalpel back into the kit the flight medic beside her was holding.

'One try.' She nodded. 'But it has to be fast.'

Cade nodded. They could do fast. There

was already a sling around the top of the car-sized boulder with a rope attached that they'd used to try and move it earlier and he'd been sitting here long enough to get an idea of where the fulcrum point might be which was the best place to put long crowbars in and then try and lever it up. Who knew, maybe the increased pressure of water from this rising creek level would work in their favour as well? But would a group of emergency service personnel who'd never met him before today trust him to issue orders and give this a red-hot crack?

Apparently, the answer was yes. Cade had never shouted as many orders as loudly as this in such rapid succession and the last one was directed to where Dr Bishop was still standing beside the rock, ready to leap in at any moment and do the amputation if their patient's condition deteriorated.

'Move right back,' he told her. 'And I mean *right* back. If this rock moves, I don't know what direction it's going to go in and I certainly don't want you underneath it.'

She didn't hesitate to obey the command. And everyone else moved the instant Cade had counted down. Two men put their full weight on the crowbars as levers. Everyone who had been able to get close enough to grip a section of the rope started pulling. Another two people were waiting in case Cade needed extra muscle power to try and pull Kayla free.

And the rock shifted. Tilted. Its position in the creek bed didn't move but the gap between the rocks widened. Just enough for Cade to feel that Kayla's leg was not being crushed. Enough that he could pull her free, only needing the assistance of those behind him to help him keep his balance as he lifted her and then negotiated slippery stones and the froth of shallow rapids to get his precious burden safely to the bank of the creek.

He was as stiff as a board after sitting so still in that water for so long and his hands were so cold he couldn't have contributed to the task of stabilising Kayla enough to get her down to the helicopter, no matter how much he wanted to, but it didn't matter. There was more than enough medical expertise on hand. Geoff had a foil sheet ready to wrap over his shoulders and his own coat got taken off Kayla and handed back to him to provide another layer. It would have been sensible to get back to their ambulance and put the heating on full bore for the trip back into the city, but Cade wasn't about to walk away from a patient he'd been holding in his arms for rather a significant amount of time.

A young woman he'd promised that he wouldn't allow to die.

So he watched the swift but thorough assessment that Dr Jo Bishop gave Kayla and the expert way she realigned the badly broken bones in her lower leg and then splinted them safely before they carried Kayla down the track. Both the tibia and fibula were obviously fractured and severely displaced and although—miraculously—the broken bones hadn't punctured the skin and created an open wound, the foot looked as if it had been without a blood supply for some time. Too long, perhaps?

He followed the basket stretcher down the muddy track and found himself walking beside Jo.

'There's still a chance she might lose that foot, isn't there?'

She nodded. 'There were no limb baselines that I could see or feel. But you know what they say…' There was a tilt to the corner of her mouth as she looked up at Cade. 'Nobody's dead until they're warm and dead so maybe that can apply to a foot as well. How cold that water was might have been protective. *Oh…*'

The alarmed squeak was caused by the sudden slide in a muddy section of the track, but Cade was quick enough to catch her before she fell. Jo was clinging to his arm with both hands as he stopped so that she could regain her balance.

'Thanks.' The smile morphed into a grimace as she let go of his arm. 'I'd better stop talking and watch where I'm walking, hadn't I?'

Cade didn't say anything, maybe because his brain was too busy absorbing the feel of her holding his arm. It didn't matter how cold he was himself, it was impossible that he could have felt the body heat that seemed to have come through the thick waterproof fabric of his coat. But there it was. He could *still* feel it, in fact.

Like the way he'd been able to feel that jolt of electricity when he'd first caught her gaze.

There was something about this woman.

Something beyond simply intriguing.

Jo waited while the flight paramedics got Kayla secured into the back of the helicopter before she climbed on board and it was a moment that gave Cade an opportunity he couldn't pass up. He helped himself to a pen clipped into a pocket of her flight suit overalls and then picked up her hand. Every paramedic knew how useful gloves were for writing on when there was no paper available. Jo was too startled to take her hand away. Maybe she'd seen something in his face. Or was it an effect of that quick persuasive grin he'd offered? Anyway, the string of numbers took only a second or two to write.

'My number,' he told her. 'I'd love a follow up on this case.'

He held her gaze a moment longer. Long enough to let her know that it wasn't just the case that Cade would love to follow up on, but it wasn't long enough to get a gauge on whether she was remotely receptive—or available to be, for that matter—to the unspoken invitation. The rotors on the helicopter were gaining speed and she was being signalled from inside the clamshell doors.

It was only after she'd turned to run, ducking her head as she got beneath the rotors, that Cade realised he'd stolen her pen.

He was smiling as he clipped it into his own pocket. It would be rude not to return the item as soon as possible, wouldn't it?

'No...' Hanna's distinctive green eyes became very wide. 'He actually promised that he wouldn't let her die?'

'He did.'

Jo took an appreciative sip of the excellent glass of sangria she had in her hand, closing her eyes as she did so. This had undoubtedly been the most dramatic anniversary of her birthday ever. It had also been a very long day and she'd only just warmed up after standing in that freezing creek for so long. She and Hanna were late for their dinner but the restaurant had kindly held their table when they knew the reason why.

A long tress of bright auburn hair got flicked over Hanna's shoulder. 'Bit unprofessional to be making a promise he couldn't be sure that he'd be able to keep, don't you think?'

Jo still had her eyes closed. 'Oh, I don't know... If I was about to die I might rather go out thinking that the man who was holding me in his arms was going to make sure I stayed alive.'

'At least he didn't promise that she wouldn't lose her leg.'

'But she didn't in the end.' Jo opened her eyes, shelving the surprisingly pleasant thought of being held like that. 'And it was Cade's idea to have one more attempt to pull her out. I have to admit, I was impressed.'

'Cade...' Hanna wriggled her eyebrows. 'Sounds like a sexy cowboy. Did you exchange phone numbers as well as introductions?'

Another sip of sangria was a good cover for not encouraging Hanna along that train of thought. Jo knew how much she would enjoy knowing that Cade had, indeed, provided his phone number and that after she'd texted him, just before heading to the restaurant, to pass on the information that the surgery on Kayla's leg had been successful, he'd responded by saying he'd love to hear more. Over a coffee or drink some time, perhaps? That text was still unanswered. Because it had been a little disturbing how tempting it had been to respond?

'It was an emergency callout, not a blind date.' Jo's tone was dismissive. 'For heaven's sake, he might be married with three kids.'

Highly unlikely, mind you. Jo might have only just met the man but instinct told her that he was very unlikely to be the type to cheat on any woman in his life. Snatches of the impressions she'd gathered were easy to retrieve. The solidness of him. The calm control of a tense situation as he'd directed that attempt to free Kayla. The tattoo. That watch... And something that she could sense in retrospect that was also purely instinctive. That Cade was a bit of a loner? A maverick?

'But if he wasn't?' Hanna's tone was teasing. She wasn't about to let this go.

'I still wouldn't be interested,' Jo said firmly. 'I'm over the effort it takes to get to know someone well enough, only to discover it's a dead end. Been there, done that way too many times, as you well know. Ooh...' It was a relief to be able to change the subject. 'Looks like our food's coming. Don't know about you but I'm *starving*. That helicopter callout made me miss lunch and then I totally forgot about it.' Jo lifted her glass and shifted cutlery to help make space as the first offerings of a smorgasbord of small bowls and platters were arranged on their table. 'This looks amazing...'

It was a delicious meal. For some time the two friends focused on sharing and tasting all the dishes. Tiny arancini balls, patatas bravas, chorizo with mushrooms in a tomato sauce, calamari and prawns. The food was good enough for Hanna to have totally forgotten to tease Jo about the impressive man she'd met today. It wasn't enough, however, for her to have forgotten about something else.

'So...what was it you were going to tell me about? Your big secret...?'

'I can't remember.' It was Jo's turn to

tease Hanna. 'The surgery on that leg fracture today? The repair of the blood vessels
was awesome. There's a big screen in Theatre and everyone can see what the surgeon
sees through his magnifying glasses. Knowing how passionate you are about emergency
medicine, I know you would've loved it.'

Hanna was giving her a long-suffering
look.

'It was so satisfying to see that foot finally
getting some colour back into it. Hopefully
there's no lasting nerve damage and she'll
get full function back…' Jo's words trailed
off into a sigh. 'Okay…okay… I'll tell you.'
She shrugged. 'It's no big deal, really. It's
something that got popular for a while, that's
all. Especially for single women in their mid
to late thirties.'

Hanna was blinking. 'What? Online dating? Speed dating? Paying for an introductory service? One-night hook-ups?'

Jo shook her head. 'Freezing your eggs.'

Hanna's jaw dropped. 'You *did* that?' She
looked slightly disconcerted. 'And there I
was thinking we were soulmates who never
had the slightest inclination to become parents.'

Jo shrugged. 'Seemed like a good idea at
the time. I was over thirty-five and I knew

how much my fertility would have already dropped. I thought if I hadn't found a partner by the time I was forty I'd seriously think about having a baby on my own.'

Hanna grimaced. 'Rather you than me.' She reached for the jug of sangria to refill their glasses.

'And then forty came and went,' Jo continued, 'and I was far too busy with my career and enjoying it too much to want to give it up and now…well…it might already be too late.'

'Hmm…' Hanna had picked up her phone and was already busy scrolling through whatever she was searching for online. 'Oh, my goodness. Did you know Janet Jackson had a baby when she was fifty? And here's a supermodel who had her first baby at forty-eight.' She was scrolling more quickly. 'It says it's more difficult to conceive naturally after forty-five but not impossible and you might need reproductive assistance but…' Hanna put down her phone. 'You're already halfway there, aren't you? You've got your eggs, which has to be the hardest part.'

'It was quite a big deal,' Jo admitted. 'I had to inject myself with hormones to stimulate as many eggs as possible and then it was a fairly invasive procedure to harvest them.'

'How many have you got in the freezer?'

'Six.'

'So all you need is a sperm donor.'

'Mmm…'

'Can I help you choose? Do you get a catalogue or something—with mug shots?' Hanna was grinning. 'Maybe it's an app these days and you can swipe right or left?'

'I have no idea. I expect a medical history and educational qualifications are deemed more important and I doubt they'd encourage people to go by looks to choose the father of their baby. It's probably not allowed, anyway. The donors are supposed to stay anonymous so they wouldn't want to be recognised by someone coming down the street pushing a pram, would they?'

'Yeah…and you're right about going by what someone looks like. I guess nobody wants to be accused of trying to create a designer baby.'

'Mind you, isn't that what you're doing when you choose a partner in real life?' Jo was frowning. If she was really going to go ahead with this, perhaps it was time to start thinking seriously about it. 'You get attracted to someone for lots of reasons and what they look like is part of that initial attraction, isn't it?'

'Totally. You're not going to set up a questionnaire about a guy's medical history before you decide whether or not to fall in love with him.'

'There are things that would never show up on paper about someone.'

'Like what?' Hanna fished a slice of orange from her glass of sangria to taste.

'Like the qualities that make someone outstanding. Courage, for example. Or compassion. You might think someone's compassionate if there's evidence of their contributions to a charity or volunteer work, I guess, but you wouldn't really know how they felt about it, would you?'

Not like seeing someone who was prepared to sit in icy water to hold onto someone who was frightened for their life. Who would promise them that he wasn't going to let them die, even if it might turn out to be a white lie.

'So you'd want to meet the donor and interview them?'

'I'm quite sure that's not going to happen. Sperm banks probably have to guarantee anonymity.'

'So you haven't checked on the rules and regulations?'

'No...' Jo sighed again. 'I did think about

it a few years ago but then it went into the "too hard" basket.'

'Until now.'

'Until now,' Jo agreed.

'Because it's now or never.' Hanna raised her glass. 'Here's to now. Happy birthday, Jo. And, you know what?'

'What?'

'While it's not something I know—or would ever want to know—anything about, my gift to you is that I'm going to help you find a baby daddy.'

Jo laughed. 'How, exactly?'

'We're going to make a list of exactly what you're looking for. Social networks are amazing things these days. Who knows? If you put it out there, something might just click. I heard a story a while back about some guy that went around in his camper van and made himself available to women who were just looking for a sperm donor.'

'No…' Jo shook her head. 'Really?'

But Hanna was busy smoothing out a clean napkin. She found a pen in her bag. 'Shoot,' she told Jo. 'What's the most important thing about the man whose sperm you want?'

Weirdly, the first thing Jo thought of was not a particular quality. It was more like a whole package of desirable traits. Wrapped up to look remarkably like Cade Cameron? She shook the image away.

'GSOH?' Hanna prompted.

'What's that?'

'Good sense of humour. You really haven't done the online dating thing at all, have you?'

Jo shook her head. 'Been too busy for that too. Have you?'

'Of course. But I gave it up a long time ago and we won't go into that tale of woe tonight. We're talking about you. Or, rather, what you want in the father of your baby.'

'Intelligence,' Jo decided. 'He doesn't have to have a PhD but if there's no way of having a conversation with them, I guess you'd have to look at what they do for a living.'

Hanna was nodding. 'You don't get to be a nuclear physicist or a brain surgeon without being reasonably clever.'

Or a critical care paramedic, Jo thought. She knew the years of training and experience that were behind that qualification were easily on a par with graduating from medical school.

'Resilience,' she added. 'The ability to face adversity and not throw in the towel.'

'Bit harder to judge.' But Hanna wrote it

down. 'And what was it you said before? Ah, yeah…compassion. And courage.'

And there it was again. The memory of Cade sitting in that water. Protecting his patient. Oh…and that cheeky grin he'd given her when he'd stolen her pen and grabbed her hand to write his phone number on her glove. There was mischief there, which suggested a sense of humour. There was also a confidence that was also attractive.

Oh, help…that was what this was all about, wasn't it?

Jo was attracted to him.

Seriously attracted. And by a lot more than merely good looks.

Hanna had finished her sangria. She eyed the empty jug. 'Shall we get another one?'

'Is that wise?'

'I start my days off tomorrow. And you're heading off to speak at that emergency medicine conference in Melbourne, aren't you? What time's your flight?'

'Not till ten.'

'You can sleep in then. This list might take a while.' Hanna was grinning as she pushed back her chair. 'I'll order the sangria on my way back from the loo. Oh…' She turned back a moment later. 'Did you catch up with the news that the ambulance bay baby got named after you?'

'No way, really?'

'Yep. Someone told the parents that it was your birthday and they were thrilled. It's officially Joseph, but they're calling him Joey. Cute, huh?'

Oddly, it was something way deeper than cute. Jo found herself blinking back tears as Hanna disappeared into the bathroom because she was back in that moment, holding that newborn baby in her arms and feeling the flood of that warmth. There was something else there now that Jo recognised from long ago. Something she had developed as a child when she'd identified something that her brothers could do but she couldn't. Like riding a bike or surfing or winning academic prizes.

A certainty that this was what she wanted, along with an absolute determination to make it happen. But this time there was also a yearning that was so strong it was almost painful. Having a baby might be totally different to any goal she'd ever set herself before, but it also seemed more significant. Something her life would not be complete without.

And…maybe…

Well, it wasn't totally beyond the realm of possibility, was it? Okay, maybe this was just in her imagination, thanks to experiencing a level of attraction she'd almost forgotten existed, but perhaps it wasn't a coincidence that fate had dropped Cade Cameron into her life on this particular day? That this was an opportunity she might be unwise to ignore?

She had nothing to lose if it was a dead end.

And it might be fun to find out. Kind of like a birthday gift to herself.

Jo pulled out her phone. She didn't have much time before Hanna got back from the bathroom but she only had to find the last text message she'd received. The one suggesting that they meet for a coffee or drink.

She tapped 'reply'.

Saturday afternoon good for you?

Jo added a smiley face.

I think you might have my pen.

CHAPTER THREE

It was Saturday afternoon.

Cade Cameron could have been right on time for their arranged meeting place outside the main entrance to the Princess Margaret Hospital, which was quite a walk from the emergency department, but Joanna Bishop knew for a fact that he wasn't there waiting for her. A swift glance at the nearest clock revealed that she was a couple of minutes late to finish her shift, but all she needed to do was sign this prescription for her last patient and then it would only take another minute or two to change out of her scrubs. Perhaps Cade simply didn't like having to wait?

The ambulance bay entrance to the emergency department was probably the one he was most familiar with, having been on duty while Jo had been out of the country for a couple of days, but it hadn't occurred to her that he might come looking if she wasn't in the arranged place. She wouldn't have expected a paramedic to use an entrance that was inappropriate when he wasn't working either, so she was taken completely off guard by his arrival.

Not just by the somewhat dramatic entrance he was making either—a lone figure walking in as the double doors obediently slid open to admit him—looking as if he'd just stepped out of some blockbuster action movie for a break.

No… Jo was thrown off-balance because she hadn't expected him to look quite so… what…intimidating?

Drop dead gorgeous?

She'd known he was tall. She'd known he was dark. But, even given the focus she'd had on their trapped patient a couple of days ago and the challenging conditions the environment had presented, how on earth had she failed to notice just how devastatingly good looking this man was?

He was dark from head to toe. Black wavy hair that was long enough to be almost touching his shoulders. A black leather jacket that could be vintage RAF, with its sheepskin lining visible. Black jeans. Black boots. A black motorbike helmet under his arm.

A serious expression on his face.

'Dr Bishop?'

'Um…yes?'

'I do believe this is yours.' Cade reached inside his jacket and then presented Jo with a ballpoint pen.

Her lips twitched but she suppressed the smile. 'Thank you.'

Jo took the pen, her gaze locked on his. Cade had to be just as aware as she was that every single person currently in this department, including patients that weren't screened by curtains, was staring at them. Jo couldn't ignore what a juicy bit of breaking news it would provide for the hospital grapevine that the emergency department HOD was about to go on what could only be deemed a date with the hot new paramedic in town and the potential for embarrassment was also taking her off guard. What *had* she been thinking when she'd responded to that text invitation?

Of course he was aware. Of the risk of embarrassing her as well as their audience. She could see the gleam of both mischief and amusement in those very dark eyes of his.

'No worries.' An eyebrow quirked. 'Gotta go,' he said calmly. 'I'm meeting someone for a coffee date. Catch you later, maybe.'

'Mmm…' The sound was slightly strangled. He was making their rendezvous private, which was exactly how she wanted it to be. But it seemed to have just become a secret between the two of them. As if they were doing—or going to do—something more than a little bit naughty.

And heaven help her, but any regret about accepting that invitation had just evaporated to make room for a flash of the kind of anticipation that almost took her back to childhood—when something was different enough to be on a whole new level of exciting.

'Nice…'

Jo tucked her hair behind her ears, the spark in her eyes telling Cade that she was trying to decide whether his hum of approval was a sarcastic reference to her finally showing up to where he was leaning against one of the pillars that framed the hospital's main entrance. He held her gaze just a heartbeat longer. It wasn't just to make sure she knew he understood perfectly well that not finishing on time was part and parcel of the jobs they both did. No… The urge to hold that gaze was also there because he wanted to test what he'd suspected a short time ago when they were being watched so intently by everyone in ED—that they could communicate rather well without saying a word.

'Great outfit,' he added, even though he knew she wasn't at all put out now. 'It's good that you're not wearing a skirt.'

He couldn't help another glance at those long, slim legs of hers, encased in faded denim that was tucked into knee high boots. Very nice…

'I don't do skirts.' Jo shrugged and then grinned at him. 'I was such a disappointment to my mother. I refused to wear dresses or play with dolls. She said it was cosmic punishment for finally getting the girl she wanted after having four sons, only to have her turn out to be a tomboy.' Her smile faded. 'Why it is good?'

'I've found what looks like the best place for us to have coffee,' Cade told her. 'And I thought you might be up for a ride there on my bike. I've got a spare helmet and jacket.'

'As a specialist in prehospital emergency medicine, I'm sure you know as well as I do how dangerous motorbikes are.'

It was Cade's turn to grin back at her. He was liking a lot more than her outfit. And he could read her real answer in her eyes as clear as day.

'So…you're up for it, then.'

A statement, rather than a question. And it felt as if it was an effort for Jo to break the eye contact with him.

'Sure…why not? It's been a busy shift and I could do with blowing a few cobwebs away.'

The Triumph Scrambler motorbike was Cade's pride and joy, so it was gratifying to see the genuine appreciation on Jo's face when she saw it.

'Very cool.' She nodded. 'Cross country?' Then her eyes widened. 'Twelve hundred CC?'

'I like a bit of grunt.' Cade raised an eyebrow. 'You know bikes?'

'I've got four brothers. How could I not know bikes? I rode one myself until I got a bit older and wiser.'

Somehow that didn't surprise Cade one bit. He could imagine this woman on the open road with the wind on her face, revelling in the freedom a bike could offer. He opened the shell case on the luggage rack and took out a leather jacket, old enough to be butter soft, holding it out for Jo to slide her arms into the sleeves. Weirdly, helping her to put an item of clothing on felt as intimate as it might be to help her take one off.

Oh, man…

He'd been looking forward to seeing Joanna Bishop again, but he certainly hadn't expected that being this close to her would feel *this* good. Even better, he was about to surprise her and he had a feeling that she might really enjoy something a bit out of the ordinary.

It was quite a tight squeeze, sandwiched between Cade's body on the front of the seat and the luggage box on the back rack, but Jo didn't mind a bit.

After a moment of feeling awkward as she put her arms around Cade's waist and felt the solid shape of his lower body against hers, she decided she might as well enjoy it. She was enjoying it so much she didn't even notice the direction that Cade was taking. She would have expected him to head for one of the trendy cafés up in the hill suburbs that gave fabulous views over the largest city in New Zealand's South Island, with its pretty harbour and the peninsula that sheltered it but, having started on the motorway that could have eventually taken them all the way to Invercargill at the bottom of the south island, Cade then turned towards the coast.

She was being abducted, Jo thought.

Whisked off to who knew where, with a man who was almost a complete stranger. For coffee…

Yeah, right… Jo actually laughed out loud as she felt the bike leaning sideways to accelerate around a bend.

'All good?' The wind whipped the words from Cade's mouth as he turned his head. 'We're almost there.'

Really? They were well past any picturesque beachside cafés that Jo knew about. Sure enough, when Cade turned off the road, there was no hint that a good espresso machine might be nearby. Instead, they were in an almost deserted parking area surrounded by farmland.

'Bit of a walk,' Cade said. 'But my research suggests that it's worth it.'

'Research?' Jo decided to keep the borrowed jacket on as the brisk sea breeze had a bite to it.

'I'm the new boy in town. I always start by looking for the more interesting corners to explore. You never know what treasures you're going to find.'

'So you make a habit of it?' Jo watched as Cade took a small backpack from the luggage case and hooked a strap over his arm. 'Being the new boy in town, I mean?'

He shrugged. 'Guess so. I never stay in one place too long.'

'Because you get bored?'

'Because I don't want to miss out on things that might be the best thing I've ever found. Like a place.' It felt as if Cade was standing very still as he spoke. As if he wanted to hold her gaze like this for as long as possible. 'Or a person…'

Oh, dear Lord. That look. The sound of his voice. The isolation of wherever it was they were, with clouds scudding over a vast sky above them and the smell of sea salt in the air was all adding up to something extraordinary.

Possibly the best thing ever?

'Where are we?'

'You don't know?'

'I grew up in the North Island. I've only been here for a couple of years.'

'So you're like me, a bit of a traveller?' Cade didn't wait for a response. 'I knew we had a lot in common, Jo Bishop. This is something new for both of us then. I like that.' He held out his hand. 'Watch out for this gravel road, it looks steep enough to be slippery down there.'

It felt like the most natural thing in the world to be holding his hand as they walked towards the sea. This was definitely something new for both of them. And Jo was liking it too. A lot.

'This is Tunnel Beach,' Cade told her. 'Apparently, back in the eighteen-seventies, some rich early settler dude decided he wanted a beach where his family could swim privately.'

'I can't see a beach. It looks as if we're walking towards the edge of a cliff.'

'That's the thing. They had a tunnel hand-carved down through the cliff. Seventy-two steps and we'll be there.'

'And there's a coffee shop?'

Cade laughed. 'I said I'd found the best *place* for coffee, not the best shop.'

A decent walk and a careful scramble down damp stone steps and Jo had to agree that this was the best place for coffee she'd ever seen. They were on soft white sand, a crescent of turquoise sea with waves being ridden by surfers, the beach framed by dramatic cliffs and massive sandstone boulders that were natural works of art. There was even a waterfall.

When they'd explored from one end of the beach to the other, there was a sheltered spot in a sandstone cleft to sit in and watch the waves and it was a bonus that the narrowness of the gap meant their hips were touching when they both squeezed in. There was hot, strong coffee, just the way Jo liked it, from a Thermos that Cade had in the backpack and there were no awkward moments in a conversation that had started at the beginning of the walking track and was now flowing so freely it felt as if they'd known each other for ever.

'Did you know that Dunedin is built around seven hills? So is Rome. And Barcelona.'

'How on earth do you know that?'

'I told you, I do my research when I go somewhere new. There's lots of places that claim the seven hills thing. Edinburgh is another one, which is kind of appropriate because Dunedin is also considered the most Scottish city outside of Scotland.'

'I *did* know that. There's a statue of Robbie Burns in the centre of town in the Octagon. And I've heard people playing bagpipes there.'

Jo liked the way Cade had laughed when she told him how she'd competed so hard with her older brothers to get the attention of their father. How she'd had to do everything they did and try to do it better. How being told she couldn't do something because she was 'only' a girl made her all the more determined.

'I wouldn't let anyone call me Joanna. I wanted a boy's name because I wanted to be just like my brothers.'

'They went into medicine?'

'Two of them are surgeons, like Dad. One works in London and the other in New York. One's a firefighter and the last one works for NASA. He's a rocket scientist but don't ask me what he actually does because I don't understand any of it.'

'Somehow, I doubt that.' The look that Jo received was one of admiration. 'Impressive family.'

'Intimidating, I've been told. Maybe that's why we all suck at relationships. I've got two brothers who are divorced, one's been engaged twice but has never married and the last one seems determined to be a bachelor for the rest of his life.'

Cade's nod was approving. 'I can relate to that. Let me guess…is he the firefighter?'

'Yep.'

'And then there's you.' Cade's eyebrow lifted. 'Are you engaged, married or divorced?'

'None of the above. My poor mother's beginning to think she's never going to get a grandchild.' She shook her head. 'I suspect she's dreaming of a girl that actually wants to be girly.'

'I like tomboys,' Cade said. 'And being single is a good thing.'

Jo ignored the odd tingle at Cade's approval of tomboys. 'Why is being single a good thing?'

'Well, I doubt that we would be here, doing this, if either of us had family or relationship commitments out of our working hours.'

'That's true...'

Jo caught her bottom lip between her teeth. The burning question for her was *why* Cade was single? Putting aside his rugged, ultimately masculine physical attraction, she'd identified qualities in him during their first meeting that would make him irresistible to almost any woman whose path he'd crossed over the years. And he never stayed in one place for long? She wanted to know the reason for that as well. She'd suspected he might be a loner, but there was always a story behind a trait that no one was normally born with. But, despite the ease of the conversation between them, the questions seemed too personal to ask so she settled for something generic.

'Have you got siblings? A bunch of sisters, maybe?'

'No. No father either, but I have enough cousins and uncles to make up for that. I might be only part Pasifika but family's still…well…everything.'

Jo had to stifle her curiosity. She knew how important family was to people with Pacific Island or Maori heritage so, if Cade had such a big extended family, why did he not live closer to them? What had happened to drive him away? And did he not want a family and children of his own? If he did, then—like her—he was leaving it a bit late. He had crinkles of lines around his eyes and the kind of ease of being in his own skin that Jo associated with men mature enough to be well into their forties.

But Cade had every right to choose what he shared in the way of personal information. She already knew from their conversation during their walk towards the beach that he'd trained as a paramedic in Auckland and had later gone on to work on oil rigs and in the mines in Australia. He'd been overseas working with Médecins sans Frontières for a few years before coming back to New Zealand to do postgraduate training and become a critical care paramedic. His working history only added to the impression that he was a maverick. That he had compelling reasons that made him walk away from commitment of any kind?

It only added to the aura of this man as far as Jo was concerned. Quite apart from the crazy idea that he could be the perfect choice for a sperm donor, he was also the most compellingly attractive man she'd ever met in her life. The point of contact where their hips touched was generating a heat she could feel throughout her entire body, so it was rather ironic that she suddenly shivered. Just a subtle quiver but Cade clearly felt it instantly.

'Yeah…it's getting colder.' He was frowning as he scanned Jo's face. He reached out to pull the overlarge borrowed jacket back from where it had slipped down her shoulder and, for a heartbeat, when his thumb brushed her chin, Jo could see a flash of something in his eyes.

As if he was thinking about kissing her…

Oh…help… Jo couldn't look away. And this time the shiver that ran through her body had nothing to do with how cold it was getting as the sun went down.

It was Cade who broke that eye contact, turning to screw the cap back onto the Thermos and put it in the backpack. 'Climbing back up those steps should warm us up.'

Jo handed him the plastic mug she'd been using. 'Thank you. That was great coffee.'

'I should have brought something to eat as well.' Cade wriggled out of the space and then held out his hand to help Jo to her feet. 'Let me make that up to you by taking you out to dinner.'

Jo got to her feet and let go of Cade's hand before he could guess the effect his touch might be having. Brushing sand off her clothes and tucking herself further into the warmth of this well-worn, soft leather jacket gave her time to blink away the surprise of both the reaction her body was having to his touch and the unexpected invitation.

A second invitation.

A date on top of a date.

Was Cade feeling the same way she was? That there was a curiously urgent need to find out as much as she could about him? To share as much about herself as he could possibly be interested in? That they had wasted too much time already because they should have met each other a long time ago?

It was unlikely. But not impossible. The way he was looking at her right now suggested that, at the very least, the level of attraction between them was on a similar level.

'Sounds like a plan,' she found herself saying, as if it was no big deal to have a date on top of another date. 'I should warn you, though, walking up hills makes me super hungry.'

'No worries. We can have an eating competition if you like.'

Jo laughed. 'You sound like one of my brothers. When he was about twelve years old.'

'I remember being twelve years old. It would have been fun to have had a little sister like you.' Jo could hear the grin in Cade's voice even though she wasn't looking at him. 'What's your favourite food?'

'I tried a new Spanish restaurant the other night which was fabulous. But I like everything. French, Italian, Chinese. Or hamburgers…' Jo was still deliberately keeping her gaze on where they were heading—towards the opening of the tunnel at the end of the beach—because she didn't quite have the courage to catch Cade's gaze again so soon. Because she knew that it wouldn't be anything like the kind of look a big brother and little sister might exchange.

The idea of asking Cade if he might consider being part of her plan to have a baby was absolutely the last thing on Jo's mind. She'd even forgotten all those burning questions about why he couldn't settle long term anywhere or with any*one*. She didn't want to ask him anything right now, to be honest.

She just wanted *him*…

She needed to pull in a steadying breath. 'I *love* a good hamburger.'

Hamburgers it was.

Gourmet burgers, mind you. Full of bacon and mushrooms and blue cheese and pulled beef. One of the best burgers Cade had ever tasted. Even better, the shop was so close to his apartment that it was a no-brainer to take them home rather than sit at outside tables on a chilly evening. They sat at the small table in his kitchen rather than anywhere more comfortable because the hamburgers were so juicy they dripped, which not only made them all the more delicious but gave Cade the pleasure of watching Jo have to lick her fingers or chase droplets with her tongue when they threatened to roll down her chin.

The kitchen was as sleek and modern as the rest of this apartment—the kind of living space Cade always rented because he didn't want a property that required maintenance. Or one that he might get attached to. He'd only been living here for the last week or so but this messy meal in the small, well-appointed kitchen was making him feel as though he had really settled in.

As if this might turn out to be his favourite apartment ever.

Because it felt so incredibly vibrant right now. Because he had one of the most beautiful, intriguing women he'd ever met bumping her face with a hamburger as if it was the best meal she'd ever tasted and he was watching her like a hawk because he didn't want to miss a single glimpse of her tongue chasing a drop of juice. Or licking her lips after a sip of the bottle of red wine that was rapidly diminishing thanks to Jo's decision to get a taxi home.

Cade didn't want her to go home, mind you.

Not any time soon.

Oddly, though, this was different to any time he'd brought a gorgeous woman home in more ways than one. Normally, he'd only have had one thing on his mind and they would have been in the bedroom some time ago but, dammit…he'd never met someone that he enjoyed talking to this much. Someone who seemed to be so at ease in his company that he felt as if he'd known her for ever. Maybe it had something to do with the fact that Jo had grown up with four older brothers and was a self-declared tomboy because he did feel as comfortable as he would if he was having a night out and a few beers with one of his best mates.

The conversation was as interesting as any he'd ever had with mates, or colleagues too. Only people with the same kind of passion for emergency medicine could have a discussion about a case they'd worked on together while they were enjoying a meal. Talking about how they would have managed the amputation if it had been necessary and about the microsurgery that Jo had watched to repair that badly fractured leg. And when they weren't talking about their work they were sharing snippets of their personal lives, like hobbies.

'What's your favourite way to burn off steam? Or stay fit?'

'I've just taken up fencing,' Jo told him.

'What, on farms? Like post and rail, or sheep netting fences?'

'No.' The peal of Jo's laughter was enchanting. '*Fencing*. With swords. You know, foils and sabres.'

'Wow...' He could imagine her wearing the skin-tight outfits and the metallic vests that recorded the touch of the weapons. 'Now that's something I'd like to try.' He could almost see Jo lunging towards an opponent with a sword in one hand and the other arm in the air for balance and, heaven help him, it was the sexiest thing he could imagine any woman doing.

'Come along to a class some time. Newbies are always welcome.'

'I'd love that. What else do you like doing?'

'I also love dancing. Lindy hop—the really fast kind. Like they did in the 1930s? Now, that's a way to really keep fit. Want to try that too?'

'Nah... I'll pass on that one, thanks.' Cade was shaking his head. 'You don't do anything ordinary, do you?'

He got to his feet to find some paper towels because the serviettes that had come with the burgers were too damp to be useful any longer. He wiped his own face before turning to offer some to Jo, who was also on her feet, gathering up the wrappers their meal had come in. He was about to pass her a towel to get rid of the drip of sauce he could see at the corner of her mouth but, for some reason, his hand froze in mid-air.

Jo turned as if she could feel his gaze and then she also froze, the balled-up wrappers slipping from her hand to land silently on the table. Her lips parted so that the smear of sauce was even more visible but, instead of offering the towel, Cade found himself reaching out instead to collect it, very gently and very slowly, with the pad of his thumb. He did it without breaking the locked gaze they were sharing. And when he lifted his thumb to remove that tiny bit of sauce by putting it into his own mouth, licking it off and then taking it out as slowly as the way he'd touched Jo's lips, he saw the exact moment that desire exploded.

He saw the way her eyes darkened. The way the tip of her tongue came out to dampen her bottom lip. He could *feel* the astonishing electricity between them. There was no need to ask out loud for consent either, given the way Jo reached for him at the same time as his hand slid behind her neck and under her hair to cup the back of her head. And the way she rose up onto tiptoes so that he could find her lips with his own a nanosecond sooner than it might have otherwise happened.

Cade had never encountered a combination of softness, fierceness and heat quite like this. A conversation in the dance of pressure and the touch of tongues that was in a totally new language for him. A taste that was like liquid fire. The shock of her bare hands touching his skin under his tee shirt made it feel as if her fingers were leaving a trail like lava across the delicate skin above his hips. It actually did feel as if it was burning his nipples a moment later so he had to grab Jo's wrists. He had to try and slow things down or this was going to be over far, far too soon.

He held her gaze again as he lifted one of her hands to his mouth. He could still taste an echo of the meal they'd shared as he took a fingertip into his mouth but it was no more than a faint background to the taste of her skin. The flavour of this extraordinary woman. He was watching the way Jo's eyes drifted shut as she made a tiny sound of need. A sigh that suggested a depth of yearning he could relate to only too easily.

Okay…maybe this was going to be over

too soon but they had the rest of the night, didn't they? He swept Jo up into his arms to carry her off to his bed.

They could go slower next time…

CHAPTER FOUR

'OH, MY GOD… What on earth's going on…?'

The expression on Hanna's face made Jo completely forget what information it was she had come to the central desk to chase up. Her head swerved to see the doors sliding open to admit a stretcher with the paramedics in attendance, but Hanna was right—this was by no means the usual way a patient was brought into the emergency department.

There was only one paramedic pushing the stretcher. The other was hanging off the edge of it by balancing on the frame. He was hanging onto the side bar to steady himself with one hand and the other seemed to be gripping the neck of the patient. Not only that, the paramedic was spattered with blood and grim-faced.

'Resus One…' Jo went ahead of the stretcher fast enough to grab gloves and be putting them on by the time it came through the doors of the high-tech resuscitation area. She reached for the protection of a mask and eye shield as the lead paramedic began a handover. There was—or had been—a lot of bleeding happening here.

'Thirty-eight-year-old male. Penetrating neck injury from an explosion in a factory. I've had direct pressure on a carotid artery bleed for...' he glanced at a military style watch '...coming up to four minutes.'

'Okay. Don't move. We'll give it at least ten minutes before releasing the pressure. Preferably twenty.' Jo could see the patient was conscious. And terrified. 'We've got you,' she told him. 'We're going to take good care of you.'

The trauma team was gathering around her. 'Let's see if we can get him on the bed—but only if it doesn't increase agitation and interfere with Cade's haemorrhage control. We're going to need bilateral wide bore IV access, oxygen on and I'd like a set of vital signs, stat, please.'

Of course it was Cade. The thought that only this man could repeatedly find such dramatic ways to attract her attention was no more than a fleeting background acknowledgement. Likewise, the visceral reaction to being this close to him for the first time since the most extraordinary first date of her life couldn't be prevented but could certainly be ignored for the time being.

'I didn't want to try and get IV access on the scene,' Cade told her. He was moving carefully with his patient during the transfer to the bed and keeping his gloved fingers buried in the wound on the side of the man's neck, despite the man's agitation and attempts to move away from pressure that was probably painful. 'Not when we were so close to ED. He's had significant blood loss. I'd estimate there was at least a litre on the factory floor and, while the first aiders had known to put pressure on the wound, they were using a folded towel and it probably soaked up another litre. There was projectile arterial bleeding again when the pad was lifted as we came through the door.'

So this patient had lost possibly thirty percent of his blood volume, which would put him in the second most severe degree of hypovolaemic shock. No wonder he was looking so pale and sweaty and was clearly breathing more rapidly than normal. The agitation was part of that as well and the sooner they had IV access to administer both pain relief and sedation, the better. Staff were moving fast around the bed now, cutting clothing clear and attaching monitoring equipment like ECG electrodes and a blood pressure cuff. Cade used his free hand to help get an oxygen mask in place, keeping up a running commentary to let his patient know what was happening around him and to reassure him. An IV trolley was being wheeled close on the other side of the bed and the airway doctor in the trauma team had a stethoscope on the man's chest already.

'Any other injuries? Was he KO'd?' Jo could see that the member of the trauma team tasked with circulation was frowning as he tried to find a vein that could be used for a wide bore cannula.

'No head injury or loss of consciousness. GCS was fourteen on arrival due to non-orientation to time or place. He's got increasingly agitated since.' Cade turned his head to make eye contact with his patient again. 'You're doing great, Bruce. Dr Bishop's right. We've got this, okay?'

Jo ordered some morphine and fentanyl to be drawn up. They could get some intramuscular medication on board to deal with the patient's pain and anxiety until they could get the IV access they needed.

'Any past medical history we should know about? Allergies?'

'No. Poor guy was just in the wrong place at the wrong time. Caught some shrapnel from the inside of a machine that spat the dummy.'

'Blood pressure's fifty-six over twenty-two,' a registrar reported. 'Heart rate one-twenty.'

Jo could see the rapid spikes of the ECG trace on the monitor's screen. She could also see that the oxygen saturation in Bruce's blood was low at ninety four percent. Their first priority was fluid resuscitation to maintain adequate perfusion for vital organs but that needed to be balanced against the risk of disrupting clots or increasing blood loss by raising the pressure. A degree of low blood pressure was preferable at this point in time. But not this low.

'Let's get some bloods off, please,' she ordered. 'I want a haemoglobin, electrolytes, group and cross-match.' She also wanted an arterial blood gas measurement as soon as possible and they'd need to get a catheter into their patient to monitor urine output. And it was taking too long to get IV access suitable for rapid infusion of fluids.

'I'm going to get a central venous line in.' She met Cade's gaze. 'Can you stay put until I'm scrubbed and we're set up? I'll go subclavian rather than external jugular so we won't get in your way. I'd prefer it to be closer to twenty minutes pressure on that wound before we test whether things are stable. I'd rather not risk switching you out for someone else before then or we might be back to square one.'

Cade ended up staying where he was long enough for both the central line and peripheral venous access to be put in place and a rapid infusion of a saline bolus to be started. The technology to monitor blood pressure internally was working and levels were already rising, thanks to the increased fluid volume. Packed red blood cells were being readied for infusion. Oxygen saturation was improving and the heart rate slowing a little as the patient's condition was stabilised and arrangements were made to take him to have a CT scan of his neck prior to being taken to Theatre.

Finally, it was time for Cade to release the pressure he'd been keeping on the carotid artery and for everybody to hold their breath, waiting to see if a spurt of blood would indicate that this crisis was not yet under complete control.

Jo breathed a sigh of relief along with everyone else in Resus when there was no sign of breakthrough bleeding but it was only after the bed was being wheeled out, surrounded by several members of the trauma team, to go to Radiology for the scan that she switched her focus, turning to where Cade was finishing his paperwork so that he could leave the patient's copy to go in the notes. His crew partner had already taken the stretcher away to clean it.

'You've been exposed to a lot of blood spatter,' she told him. 'Maybe I should take some blood and check your antibodies for HIV and hepatitis.'

'I'm vaccinated for Hep A and B. Unless something shows up in Bruce's bloodwork, I think I'm good.'

'You've got blood on your arms. Have you got any broken skin?'

'Not that I know of.'

'Let me check…' Most of the trauma team had gone already, either to CT with their patient or back to other positions in ED, but there was a nurse tidying up discarded packaging and a technician wiping down equipment. Not that there was anything unprofessional about Jo touching Cade's bare arms below his uniform sleeves to see if he had any obvious cuts or grazes that could present a hazard for blood borne diseases.

It just felt really, really personal.

Maybe that was because she could see the lower part of Cade's tattoo and she knew perfectly well that the waves and swirls of the traditional Polynesian design covered his whole upper arm and extended onto both his back and his chest. And because, despite the gloves she was wearing, she could feel the heat of his skin and that took her straight back to Saturday night.

She'd never had a date like that in her life. Ever.

She'd never talked so much about herself during the first part of their time together. Or eaten messy food, not caring that it was dripping all over her face. She'd definitely never even considered going to bed with someone on a first date, let alone losing count of how many times they'd had sex.

Okay, that wasn't quite true. She knew exactly how many times. Three. But only if you counted that first explosive release that was more about sheer lust than the delicious exploration and pleasure of the lovemaking that came later.

Jo didn't dare look up to meet Cade's gaze as she scanned the bare skin of his arms with such unprofessional thoughts flashing through the back of her mind, but she had to look up to check the rest of the unprotected skin on his face.

'Were you wearing a mask and eye shield?'

'Yes. We knew we were going to a serious blood loss incident. I took them off when I was confident I had things under control. I hate it when the plastic starts fogging up.'

'Hmm.' Jo knew she should impart a bit of professional advice about the use of PPE but Cade was smiling at her and…and she was losing her train of thought.

He'd texted her the day after that astonishing date. Just a smiley face, but it had been enough to suggest that he was thinking about her. About the sex? And that thinking about either or both of those things was enough to make him happy…

She'd texted him and offered an invitation to join her in a fencing class because he'd said he'd like to try the sport, but he'd been working an unexpected night shift to cover a colleague whose wife had gone into labour. She hadn't texted him yesterday because she knew he'd be sleeping after the night shift so this was the first time they'd seen each other since Saturday. It was all very well sending a smiley face to suggest that Cade had been feeling good after his time with her. It was quite another thing to see the warmth that was lighting up his eyes in a silent message that no one else could possibly be aware of.

He looked as though he would be really happy to see her again—out of work hours. Somewhere private…

And heaven help her, but Jo was suddenly having trouble thinking about anything else herself.

'Um… I can't see any broken skin,' she murmured. 'I'd recommend you have a shower as soon as possible, though, and get out of that contaminated uniform.'

Oh…there was more than a gleam in those dark eyes now. There was a cheeky grin simmering in the background as Jo got the message that there was plenty more skin she would be welcome to inspect but, again, it was a secret communication.

'I'll do that,' was all he said aloud, as a nurse came in with a sterile pack in her arms that was probably a replacement central venous line kit. 'Thanks, Doc.'

'No worries. If you're back in later on your shift, come and find me. I'm sure you'll want to see the CT results on your patient. You saved a life today.'

It always felt good to know that you'd made a positive difference to someone's life, let

alone saving it, whether or not it got ac-
knowledged by others. It was even better,
however, when it got noticed by someone
like Joanna Bishop. Cade might have only
been working in this city for a week or so but
he was already getting a feel for the medical scene. He was rapidly learning which
rest home he'd choose for his mother due
to the high standard of care and which GP
was notable for a less than acceptable standard. He'd met colleagues whose opinion
and skills he could respect and staff in the
emergency department that were on top of
their game. None more so than the head of
department, however, so winning Jo's respect for his work really meant something.

Winning her interest on a personal level
was a completely unexpected bonus but the
frequency with which Cade found himself
thinking about Jo was a warning not to let
it become too significant, which was why
he hadn't texted her since Sunday evening,
when he'd had to decline her invitation to try
out a fencing class. It wasn't that he didn't
want to see her again, it was simply that he
was playing it cool. At some point, preferably as soon as possible, he needed to have
the conversation that he always had with any
women who'd shared any part of his life in

the last ten years. The one where he made sure they were on the same page and that this was never going to be anything more than a friendship. Spending time with Jo could become a very enjoyable part of his life outside working hours when or if it suited them both but it had to stay casual.

Fun.

As much fun as the game of keeping it to themselves in a professional environment was turning out to be? Yeah…especially when he suspected Jo was enjoying it as much as he was.

Okay, maybe he was leaning a little closer than he should have when she was showing him the CT scan results on the carotid artery injury later that day, having spotted him when he'd been on his way out of the department, but she was using the small screen of a tablet and he needed to be close enough to see properly.

'So you can see the shadow of the foreign body, with metallic density, here at the carotid sheath space.'

'Good grief… I'm kind of glad I didn't know it was there. I might have thought twice about how much pressure I put on his neck.'

'He'd be dead if you hadn't stopped the

bleeding.' Jo scrolled into another file. 'They did CT angiography before he went to Theatre and they found multiple traumatic pseudoaneurysms of the left internal carotid artery.' Her head was bent as she peered at the screen. 'Look... Can you see that? There? And...there?'

'Yep. Hmm.' Oh, he was close enough to smell Jo's skin. And he knew exactly how soft that particular spot at the nape of her neck was. He also knew it was a very effective erogenous zone for Jo. Cade had to clear his throat before speaking again. 'I could imagine that that would have taken some fixing.'

'They used a shunt, blocked the external carotid artery, resected the pseudoaneurysm, removed the fragment of metal and then stitched everything up. Patient's doing well so far but he's in ICU for monitoring.'

'I might come back when I've finished my shift and see if I can visit him. I wonder if Kayla's still an in-patient. I could pop in and see how she's doing as well.'

'Let's check.' Jo accessed an inpatient data base on the hospital's intraweb. 'No,' she said moments later. 'Kayla got discharged over the weekend. But the discharge summary sounds positive. Good movement in her toes and any nerve damage causing lack of sensation may resolve in time. She's non-weightbearing until they review her in Out-patients when she comes in to get a more lightweight cast.' She tucked her hair behind her ear as she glanced up to smile at Cade. 'You have a bit of a talent for being involved in memorable cases, don't you? Kayla and now today's drama. Everyone's still talking about the way you rode in on that stretcher. I've heard the word "cowboy" a few times.'

Oh…he loved the way she tucked her hair behind her ears like that.

He loved her smile even more.

'I have always been a trauma magnet,' he admitted. 'And it's not the first time I've been called a cowboy but people seem to like working with me. Nothing like a chal-lenge or two to keep a job interesting.' He leaned even closer and lowered his voice. 'I know how to make time out of work pretty interesting too, if you don't mind a bit of the Wild West.'

To outward appearances, it would seem that Dr Bishop was focused on what she was reading on screen. In reality, she made a humming sound that made it hard for Cade to stifle a grin.

'I owe you a dinner,' she murmured. 'How 'bout I text you my address?'

Jo's small Victorian terraced house in the central city couldn't have been more of a contrast to Cade's modern apartment even though they were no more than a few blocks apart. The rooms had high ceilings with elaborate plaster cornices and roses, bay windows at the front and gas fireplaces set inside carved wooden surrounds. It was cold enough this evening to have the fires going and the real flickering flames added to the cosy ambience of the rooms.

The food Jo intended to offer for dinner was going to be rather different too. No messy, drippy hamburgers. Maybe she wanted Cade to see a different side to a woman who could appreciate street food. And, okay, maybe she hadn't had the time to make everything from scratch but the nearby upmarket delicatessen and butchery had the kind of elegant food she wanted to serve. She had a whole beef fillet and scalloped potatoes ready to go into the oven and green runner beans tied up in elegant little bundles with the edible string that chives provided.

Fortunately, she'd only just turned the oven on by the time Cade arrived, with a bottle of excellent red wine under his arm. Because while the décor and food might be very different from the Saturday evening they'd spent together last weekend, one thing was exactly the same.

That astonishingly fierce desire for each other. Sexual tension like nothing Jo had ever discovered. There was no way they were going to sit down and eat dinner any time soon. They couldn't even do more than taste the wine.

'I think you'll like this,' Cade said, handing her a glass. 'It's one of my favourites.'

Jo tasted the wine, made an appreciative sound and then looked up at Cade as she licked her lips, to find his gaze fixed on her mouth. She heard the way he released his breath in a silent whistle and it was as eloquent as if he'd said what was foremost in his mind. His action of taking the glass back from her hand and putting it down on the table beside his own was also a clear message of his intent but Jo didn't mind him taking charge like this.

For someone who'd always rebelled against being told what to do, she actually liked it far more than she should have.

She was ready for the touch of Cade's hand on her neck, just lightly, on that sensitive spot on her nape before he slid his fingers up into her hair. It was instinctive to lean into that touch. To tip her head back, which also made her close her eyes. That way, she was ready to experience the shock of pleasure as his lips covered hers, simply through touch and taste. Hearing got added with that grunt of bliss that came from Cade as his tongue joined the party. And smell was there as a background, of course. This man had the most amazingly fresh masculine scent, but there was also a raw musky tone that was pure sex and utterly irresistible.

They stopped at the foot of the narrow staircase at the end of the hallway to kiss again. Shoes got kicked off and an item or two of clothing got discarded on the stairs before they reached Jo's bedroom and then she discovered that something else was different about tonight.

The sex was different.

Better.

Because, already, there was a familiarity that made things more comfortable and gave them both more confidence to initiate—and respond to—everything every sense, including sight, could offer them.

And as Jo lay in Cade's arms some time

later, catching her breath, she realised that there was something she'd never found this early on in any relationship she'd had over so many years—a feeling of trust… Which was weird because that was something that had become harder and harder to find as the years, and failed relationships, had gone by. She'd barely met Cade but there seemed to be a connection here that was completely new.

And very, very different.

Perhaps that was because she'd made such a huge decision the day she'd met Cade. She might be planning to have a baby but, as she'd told Hanna, she'd given up long ago on finding a life partner. She might have seen Cade as a perfect donor but the reason they were here together, like this, was only because she'd thought it would be fun getting to know him better.

And…wow…she hadn't been wrong. It was so good that there was a tiny voice in the back of her head suggesting that she might have stumbled across what she'd been looking for for ever. That this could be the start of a relationship that could last the distance. For ever, even?

Jo needed to silence that voice. She might be aware of a level of trust between herself and Cade but she wasn't going to allow herself to go down that well-worn track when she knew the kind of heartbreak she would find at the end. And she needed to distract whatever was behind that voice before it could come up with even more persuasive suggestions.

She twisted away from Cade's arms. 'I'd better go and rescue our dinner.'

Like everything else about Joanna Bishop, the food she served was impressive.

'Man, you can cook,' Cade told her. 'This is like restaurant quality.'

'I have a confession to make.'

'Oh?'

'All I had to do was put it in the oven for the prescribed time and steam the beans. It was really made by the deli that I walk past when I'm coming home. I can't cook to save myself.'

Cade ate in silence for a minute but he was liking this a lot. Not just that a seemingly perfect woman had flaws like any normal person but that she was happy to be honest about them.

'Your turn,' Jo told him.

'My turn for what?'

'Confessing something.' Jo eyed him over the rim of her wine glass.

Cade grinned. 'I have to confess that… I like you,' he said.

'That's your confession?' She put her glass down.

'Yep.'

Jo laughed. 'Fair enough. Okay, I like you too but I'm sure there's something more interesting about you that I don't know.'

Cade shrugged. 'I'd rather talk about you. And how you tried to outdo those poor brothers of yours? I'm guessing that's how you ended up being a head of department at such a young age.'

'Young? How old do you think I am?'

Cade swallowed another piece of the melt-in-your-mouth fillet steak. ''Bout my age?'

'How old *are* you?' Jo was spearing beans with her fork.

'Thirty-seven.'

The fork dropped with a loud clatter. 'Oh, my God.' Jo sounded horrified. 'You're kidding.'

'Is it a problem?'

'You're not even forty.'

'That's generally how it works. You have to be thirty-seven first.' He grinned at her. 'You mean you've already hit the big Four-O?'

'Some time ago. Good grief…' Jo picked up her wine glass. 'I've become a cougar.'

'As in an older woman who preys on younger guys for sex?' Cade laughed. 'As if. You don't even look forty but if you are, bring it on, I say.'

'I'm forty-six, Cade. *Nine* years older than you.'

'So what?' Cade shrugged. This was perfect. They could have the conversation he'd been intending to have without it seeming awkward at all. 'It's not as if this is anything serious.' He'd been there, done that. Never again. He didn't talk about it either, so it was a bit disturbing that he found himself wanting to tell Jo about it right now. To confess that he wasn't capable of falling in love again and…that sometimes it was a lonely way to live…

But Jo didn't need to know that and maybe he didn't want to tell her because he didn't want her to feel sorry for him. He cleared his throat.

'I told you I never stay in one place for long.' It was a well-honed protective mechanism. Never get too attached—to people or places—because it was so much easier to cope when they weren't there any longer. 'A year or two and I'll be moving on again—

that's the way I roll. As I said, I like you, Jo, and age is just a number. It doesn't make the slightest difference. Not to me.' He held her gaze. 'But maybe it does for you? If you're looking for something more…significant?'

She shook her head. He could see something in her eyes that was familiar. A bit heart-wrenching. 'I think I gave up on the idea of significant a long time ago. I've had too many dead-end relationships. I've watched too many other marriages disintegrate, including my brothers'.'

Ah…that was what it was. Jo Bishop knew about the particular kind of loneliness that came from the knowledge you were treading a path through life alone. She was clearly quite capable of doing that very successfully but Cade was aware of a vulnerability that made him want to reassure her.

To look after her—to the best of his ability—at least for a while?

'There you go, then. No wonder we get on so well. We're good together.' He raised his glass. 'Maybe we should make the most of it while it lasts?'

'I'd like that.' Jo clinked her glass against his. 'I do have another confession, though.'

'What's that?' There was a sparkle in her eyes now that he'd seen somewhere before.

Oh, no…she wasn't about to tell him that she was falling in love with him, was she?

She took a deep breath. 'I'm planning to have a baby,' she said.

Cade came very close to choking on the mouthful of wine that tried to go down the wrong way. He might have sworn a little under his breath as well. And then he shook his head.

'I've never met anyone like you,' he said. 'There's a proper confession for you.' He could feel one side of his mouth lifting into a crooked smile. 'Your mother will be delighted.'

Jo screwed up her nose. 'I'm not sure about that. She'll probably think it's irresponsible to actually plan to be a single mother.'

The odd tension Cade was experiencing dropped noticeably. Except…good grief… was this why she'd been so happy to jump into bed with him on their first date? Thank goodness he'd had a good personal supply of protection. The thought that Jo would use somebody like that didn't sit well, however. Had his instinct about her being trustworthy been misplaced? His tone was cautious when he spoke again.

'So…you're planning to get pregnant and not tell the father?'

'I think that's usually how it works for fertility clinics and donated sperm.' A flush of colour was appearing in Jo's cheeks. 'Oops... too much information.' She reached for her wine glass to drain the last mouthful.

Cade couldn't look away from her face. She really was blushing, which was kind of cute. He filed it away, with that hint of vulnerability he'd seen in her. The other side of the coin that was the extraordinarily confident, competent woman he'd been so attracted to.

He picked up the bottle of wine to refill her glass. 'Something else you might have to make the most of,' he said. 'You'll have a long stretch of going wine free soon.' He raised an eyebrow. 'Presumably soon?'

'I'm finally ready to get on with it.' Jo nodded. 'I decided last week. On my birthday. The day I met you, actually.'

'I didn't know.' Cade raised his glass in another toast. 'Happy belated birthday.'

'Thanks.'

'That's quite a present you've given yourself. It's a big decision.'

'Not a spur of the moment one, though. I had eggs frozen when I was in my late thirties. I didn't want to wake up one day and find I'd totally lost the opportunity to be a mother. It was in the wake of another disastrous relationship ending and I'd just become a consultant as well, so I knew it would be a few years before I could take time out from my career.' Jo let her breath out in a sigh. 'I have no idea why I'm telling you all this. Except that… I would like to spend more time with you, so I guess I thought it was only fair to tell you about what's going on in my life. Plus, you know… I was on a bit of a roll with those confessions.'

'I get it.' Cade looked down at his plate. There was still some of that delicious deli-bought food left, but somehow he'd lost his appetite. Something had gone very wrong with the conversation he'd been planning to have with Jo. The one where they confirmed that they were both on the same page about a no-strings, no-expectations friendship that included plenty of the best sex he'd ever had in his life?

Jo had followed his gaze. 'You've had enough?'

He nodded. 'It was great. I've just…had enough.'

'I didn't get any dessert, I'm sorry.'

'That's a good thing. And…' Cade glanced at his watch '…it's getting late anyway and

I've got a five a.m. start for my day shift. I should probably head home.'

Jo was on her feet instantly. She shook her head when Cade went to pick up his plate, however.

'Don't touch a thing. I'll take care of it. My penance for not actually cooking for you.'

Cade pulled her into his arms so that he could kiss her. 'You have talents that I appreciate even more than being able to cook.' He kissed her again. 'You're an astonishing woman, Jo Bishop. Did I tell you that I've never met anyone like you?'

She was smiling up at him. 'You did.'

'And I admire you for going after something that you want. You'll be as amazing as a mother as everything else you do in life.'

There was a sparkle in her eyes that made him think that she might be about to cry so he kissed her again before reaching for his leather jacket that he'd draped over the back of a chair and started to walk towards the door.

'Let me know if there's anything I can do to help.'

It was an automatic thing to say by way of a farewell. Stealing another kiss on Jo's front doorstep as a final goodnight was just as automatic.

'Well...you *would* make the perfect father.'

Cade's heart actually skipped a beat despite the casual tone of her words, but then Jo's face creased into an apologetic sort of smile that was almost a visible cringe.

'Just kidding....'

Cade didn't say anything. He *couldn't* say anything. Jo wasn't to know that she'd stepped onto forbidden ground. That she'd blindsided him and that his fight or flight reflex was telling him to get the hell out of Dodge. He zipped up his jacket, jammed his helmet on and fired up his bike.

It could never be a joke. When he lifted a hand as he took off on his bike he knew the gesture might later be interpreted as a final farewell.

Okay, he already knew that Jo didn't deserve to be dropped like this, and he felt bad about that, but this was another of his well-honed protective mechanisms. Never going anywhere near that forbidden ground voluntarily had been the way he'd learned to cope in the first place.

And if something wasn't broken there was no need to fix it, was there?

CHAPTER FIVE

SHE'D BLOWN IT.

Time after time, over the next week or so, Jo watched Cade come into the emergency department. She might see him talking to Hanna as she triaged the patient being brought in and, more often than not, it was a run-of-the-mill type of situation that didn't need her involvement. An elderly person with exacerbation of their COPD due to an infection, perhaps, or an abdominal pain or minor injuries from an MVA. Cade's reputation as a 'trauma magnet' who got sent to the most serious cases might be getting dented but he didn't seem bothered. He looked happy in his work and was perfectly friendly when he smiled at Jo in passing or followed up on one of his cases.

Given that they'd been so careful to keep their mutual attraction a secret, not even Hanna had any idea what Jo was thinking or feeling when she saw Cade—or worse, when he was talking to her about a case and standing close enough to make her skin prickle. When she didn't dare meet his gaze directly because she had a bit of pride and she wasn't going to let him know that she was surprisingly badly hurt.

She would never want him to know that she'd fought back tears as she'd cleaned up the meal that neither of them had finished. That she'd come even closer to being undone when his scent had filled her nostrils as she'd straightened the rumpled linen on her bed. That looking out of the window at the street as she'd pulled the curtains that evening made it impossible to stop a single tear trickling down the side of her nose, as if she could see him leaving all over again, as if she was still standing on the doorstep. Watching him disappearing into the night, with a single dismissive wave of a gloved hand.

Knowing it was her own stupid fault for even joking about something that would send any committed bachelor running for the hills didn't help because she suspected Cade had known that, on some level, she hadn't really been joking at all.

This was the flip side of that connection

that let them communicate without saying a word, wasn't it? The one that had made it so enjoyable to flirt secretly at work. Fortunately, Jo discovered it was possible to cut the line on that connection and, to outward appearances, at least, she wasn't bothered in the least. She could be just as friendly. Only yesterday, she'd sent Cade a link to an introductory session her fencing club was offering to anyone who might be interested. She'd received a smiley face in response.

Not that it made Jo smile this time. But it did give her enough of a shove in the right direction to realise that she could choose how to react to this. It didn't have to change anything. When the private disturbance had settled enough to not be messing with her head, she would simply move on and the first positive step into her future would be to make an appointment with that fertility clinic. Maybe fate had sent Cade Cameron crashing into her life to demonstrate that too much information on a sperm donor was not a good thing, after all.

She was almost at that point just a day or two later. She even had the contact details of the clinic in her phone so, when her pager went off to request a trauma specialist to go with the helicopter callout to a bad accident on a rural road, the thought that Cade might be at the other end of the flight was no problem. Jo pulled her flight suit over her scrubs, shoved her feet into the steel-capped boots she kept in her locker and ran for the lift that would take her up to the rooftop landing pad.

She hoped Cade *would* be there, for the sake of victims who might need a hero to keep them alive.

He knew it was going to be a nasty smash before they got anywhere near the scene or updates on the status of the victims. They wouldn't have dispatched a helicopter at the same time as a road vehicle unless the local fire and rescue or police personnel had advised how serious this multi-vehicle accident was. He just hoped that they wouldn't have requested the addition of a trauma specialist to the crew because he would rather not arrive to find Jo as the lead medic and he was sure she would rather not have to work with him.

He felt quite bad enough, having backed away from anything to do with her on a personal basis, and he knew damn well that he'd hurt her. It didn't seem to be getting any easier to get past that guilt as the days ticked past. If anything, he was increasingly missing what they'd discovered with each other. He knew that an opportunity had been lost to make the most of something that was rare enough to be like winning the lottery.

A lottery that you couldn't even buy tickets for.

Ironically, though, the more days that stacked up, the more out of reach any way to put things right was becoming. Cade could feel himself slipping back into a space where deeply personal communication—especially the kind that could happen when you didn't say anything aloud—was something best avoided. Which was easy when you were only with someone in a situation when something personal was the last thing on your mind.

Like when you arrived at a scene on a rural road now blocked off from normal traffic, by emergency vehicles in the direction Cade arrived from and a helicopter that had landed further up the road on the other side. There were crumpled cars in between, rescue workers in high-vis jackets crowded around the wrecked vehicles and the noise of pneumatic tools being used to gain access to their interiors, with metal popping and glass shattering. One car had a tarpaulin covering its windows.

The police officer wearing a scene commander vest told Cade that two vehicles had collided head on at high speed and a third had been collected by a car spinning onto the wrong side of the road. She confirmed that the covered vehicle had a deceased driver and passenger and that the people from the third vehicle had been triaged as being status three to four, which meant that their injuries were minor to moderate. Cade sent Geoff to reassess them. He went towards where the main drama was obviously focused on one vehicle.

Fire crews were in the process of peeling back the roof of this car and a man wearing a cervical collar and oxygen mask was in the driver's seat. A flight paramedic was in the back seat of the car, stabilising the man's neck, and they were both under a protective plastic sheet so he didn't see Cade approaching.

'Over there, mate,' a fire officer directed him. 'I reckon the doc needs some assistance.'

The 'doc'. Cade knew who it was as soon as he saw the back of the figure crouched in long grass on the verge of the road. She had her stethoscope ear pieces in and the disc on the exposed chest of a patient who was lying on a helicopter stretcher with the bright orange spinal board that would have been used to extricate him from the vehicle still beneath him. IV access had already been secured and a bag of fluids was being held aloft by a police officer who looked relieved to see Cade's arrival. Cardiac monitoring was in place but, more tellingly, the patient was already intubated and hooked up to a portable ventilator, which told Cade that his condition was critical. Had Jo managed all that by herself or had her crew partner been assisting before he climbed into that wrecked car?

It wouldn't have surprised Cade at all if Jo had already achieved major life-saving interventions without expert assistance. He knew how good she was at her job. And it only took a split second to realise how wrong he'd been in assuming that Jo wouldn't want to work with him.

'I'm so glad it's you,' she told him. 'This lad was initially responsive to voice on arrival, but became unresponsive with increasing respiratory distress as soon as we lifted him out. Correct tube placement confirmed by capnography but I'm not happy that he's stable enough to load and go.'

She didn't look happy, Cade thought. He could see a mix of complete focus and real distress in her eyes and the need to support Jo was instantly right up there with the need to do whatever he could to help with this patient. He shrugged off the strap of his backpack to put it down in the long grass.

'I think there's decreased air entry on the left side,' Jo said, 'but it's so hard to hear with the background noise. Could you have a quick look at his chest from his feet, please?'

'Sure.' Cade knelt and then leaned on his elbows so that he could be at eye level with the chest he needed to assess. This was an effective way to spot serious injuries that could be invisible when you were looking from above at either the side or head of the patient.

It was a small chest. Jo had called him a 'lad' and he was clearly no more than a child. Nine or ten years old, perhaps. Cade pushed the thought away. Hard. He focused on what he could see. Bruising that was already appearing on pale skin and…yes…he could see that a part of the chest wall was not moving the way it should. Instead of going out with a breath being drawn like the surrounding ribs, it was being drawn in and then rising as the breath was expelled.

'Paradoxical movement left side,' he told Jo.

She nodded. 'Peak pressures are rising, which is consistent with pneumothorax, and we've got some surgical emphysema happening now as well.'

Cade positioned himself on the other side of the young boy. He could see the bubbles of air under the skin that Jo was referring to. It was quite possible that, within a short amount of time, they might be dealing with a cardiac arrest due to blood and/or air accumulating within the chest and preventing the lungs from functioning despite the mechanical assistance.

They were in real danger of losing this patient.

And it took an even bigger push to get rid of that thought. This was almost too hard… Harder than it had ever been, but this wasn't the moment to wonder why that was the case.

'Needle thoracotomy?' he asked.

Jo shook her head. 'It rarely facilitates lung expansion and it's not enough for a large volume of blood or air. I'm going to do a finger thoracotomy. Quick and effective. You happy to assist?' She was pulling an equipment roll out of her kit. 'I could get Tom out of the car but that needs to be a very controlled extrication. The guy's got severe neck pain and no movement in his hands or lower limbs. It was a mission for Tom to get him calm enough for the firies to be able to get started on the car.'

'I'm good,' Cade told her. 'What do you need first?'

'I need his left arm abducted and externally rotated. And then the lateral chest wall well disinfected with chlorhexidine spray.' Jo opened her sterile kit and then stripped off her gloves to put on a new pair.

Watching Jo work dispelled any doubts about her ability to work alone. It also gave Cade too much time to think about their patient, and it had to be because he was with Jo and she'd already ventured unknowingly into that forbidden space that he found his own protective barriers crumbling. Jo was fighting to save this boy's life. Cade was fighting his own battle and he had a horrible feeling that it could be a fight he might be losing.

Something wasn't right.

Not that Jo could afford to give it any head

space but it was obvious that Cade was far from happy. She knew it didn't have anything to do with him having to work closely with her, however. He might not be deliberately trying to communicate silently with her—quite the opposite, probably—but she could sense that he was on the brink of being overwhelmed by something far more significant.

It didn't interfere with what she was doing. Creating an opening in the chest wall to deal with a life-threatening problem was a procedure she was more than simply familiar with and the steps were almost automatic. With one hand, she felt down the ribcage to locate the fifth intercostal space, keeping a finger to mark the mid-axillary line as she reached for a scalpel with her other hand. The small incision was only through the skin. She used small, curved artery forceps for blunt dissection through the intercostal muscles, over a rib and into the pleural space. Opening the forceps allowed the release of both a gush of air and blood and then Jo did a finger sweep, mindful of the hazard that the sharp edges of broken ribs could present, to ensure decompression.

'I can feel the lung expanding,' she told Cade. No matter how many times she performed this procedure, the relief that came with that feeling beneath her fingertip never got old.

They weren't about to lose this patient. Oddly, though, Jo didn't see a reflection of her own relief as Cade's gaze brushed hers and, again, she knew that this wasn't about her. She wanted to ask if he was okay, but they could both hear Tom calling for assistance. They were about to lift the adult male from the car.

'Go,' Jo told Cade. 'I'm good here.'

He couldn't get away fast enough, judging by how swiftly he jumped to his feet and turned and Jo could see him assisting Tom, moments later, as they carefully extracted the man with a potentially serious cervical injury from the wreckage. They had him immobilised with sandbags and strapping on a spinal board by the time she'd dressed the chest wound she had created and was happy with the vital signs she reviewed. A second air rescue chopper was landing so all they needed to do was transfer the man with the neck injury into the care of the other crew and they could get this boy back to her emergency department and into the care of appropriate specialists.

The patients with minor injuries could

be left to Cade and his partner to treat and transport to hospital by road, if necessary. As the lead medic at this scene, Jo needed to ensure that Cade was aware of what was happening but, when she got close enough to speak to him, moments before she needed to get back on board the helicopter, it wasn't the other patients that were foremost on her mind.

'Are you okay?' she asked him.

'I'm fine.'

He clearly wasn't. He was pale. The muscles in his face looked set in grim lines and there was something in his eyes that Jo couldn't interpret but it seemed as dark as their colour.

'You don't look fine.' She didn't need to speak quietly because the helicopter's rotors were starting up. Tom was holding the clamshell door, waiting for her to get in so he could pull it shut, but Jo hesitated for just another heartbeat, her gaze fixed on Cade's face, the squeeze in her chest on his behalf painful enough to be stealing her breath.

'Drop it, Jo.' Cade's tone was a warning. He spun around so that she was facing his back. '*Dammit…*' He actually sounded as if he was in physical pain. 'Just leave me alone, will you?'

He strode away, leaving Jo momentarily stunned by the way she'd been pushed away so viciously. But then she turned away herself almost as swiftly. She was needed on board the helicopter and it was all too obvious that Cade neither needed nor wanted her in his life.

And that was fine by her.

CHAPTER SIX

MAYBE THIS WAS a bad idea.

It was late enough to have been dark for some time. Late enough for someone to have already had their dinner and be winding down for an evening that was chilly and more than a little damp. Cade had to wonder whether Dunedin was considered the most Scottish city outside of Scotland for its weather as well as its early settlers and architecture?

Whatever. Jo probably wouldn't be remotely interested in the large bag of rapidly cooling Thai takeaways he took out of the case on the back of his bike. She probably wasn't going to be remotely pleased to find him on her doorstep at all, but what else could he do in the way of a peace offering?

The answer to that came the moment that Joanna Bishop opened her door. He could apologise with absolute sincerity.

He'd known just how far over the line he'd stepped the moment he'd turned his back on her, hours ago, at the scene of that MVA. The fact that defence mechanisms he'd relied on for so many years had suddenly disintegrated and left him feeling so vulnerable… okay, *afraid*…was no excuse to have treated Jo like that. Or like he had been treating her for the last week or more.

'I'm so sorry,' Cade said quietly. 'I don't have any excuse but I could explain if you want me to?'

Without a word, Jo led him into the house. She ignored the paper bags he put on the table. Her arms weren't completely folded but the way she was almost hugging herself was a protective gesture that made Cade feel even worse for the way he'd treated her.

'How is he?' Cade had to ask. 'The boy from the car crash? I didn't get a chance to ask anyone later.'

'He's alive. He's in ICU but considered stable now, rather than critical.'

Cade nodded slowly.

'His dad's been transferred to a specialist spinal injury unit but they think his cord injury is incomplete, which is good news. He could make a good recovery.' Jo was watching him carefully. 'It was a tough job for you today, wasn't it?'

Cade nodded again.

'Working on critically injured kids is always tough, I get that.'

Cade shook his head this time. 'I've always managed before, but yeah…it was beyond hard today but I had no right to blame you for any of it. Or take it out on you like that.'

'You *blamed* me?' Jo actually took a step backwards.

'No…that's not the right word.' Cade let his breath out in a sigh. 'Look…this isn't easy for me to talk about. Could we at least sit down?'

Silently, Jo pulled out a chair and sat down at the table, pushing the paper bags to one side. She had to be able to smell the food as well as he could but she was clearly no more interested in eating at the moment than Cade was. He also sat down, his heart sinking a bit when he remembered they were sitting in the same places when he'd had dinner here with Jo—the night things had started falling apart.

'It was what you said.' The words were hard to get out. 'That I would make a perfect father.'

Jo bit her lip. 'I'm sorry. It was a stupid thing to say.'

'You were joking.'

Jo opened her mouth as if she was about to say something else but then closed it again, pressing her lips together.

'You weren't to know,' Cade said. 'That, years ago, that was all I wanted to be. The perfect father.'

Jo's eyes widened. The rest of her went very still.

'I joined a shearing gang that my cousins were in when I left school. There was a girl in the gang—Nina—who worked as a rousie on the gang. Throwing fleeces? Anyway… long story short, we fell in love. Spent a few years travelling and then decided to settle down. Nina went into nursing training and I decided to become a paramedic. We got married—big family wedding—and then had an even bigger celebration when Nina got pregnant a year or so later. That was when I decided I was going to be the perfect father. And husband. I was already loving my work, we had a big family network and…well, life couldn't have been better.'

Jo still hadn't moved. She was waiting for what was obviously not going to be a happy ending to his story.

'There was an accident,' Cade continued quietly. 'Nina was seven months pregnant. Driving home on a rural road and a drunk driver went through a stop sign straight into the driver's side of the car. I doubt that she had any idea what hit her—at least I hope not.'

'Oh, my God...' Jo breathed. 'Cade, I'm so sorry...'

'It was the end of my world as I knew it.' Cade shrugged. 'I'd had my family torn away from me and I couldn't handle any of it. Even being around my own family was too hard. That was when I joined MSF and worked overseas. The oil rigs were good too. Anything that kept me moving was good because I couldn't get attached. To anywhere. Or anyone. I'm not saying it stopped me having fun with people I liked being around.' Cade offered Jo a slightly tentative smile. 'But there were rules.'

'I knew that.' Jo nodded. 'You made it very clear that you never stayed long in one place. If I'm honest, I wasn't really joking, I *did* think you'd make a perfect father for the baby I want to have and that was partly because you'd move on. I'm really not looking for a partner. I just...' There was a wobble in her voice that went straight to Cade's heart. 'I just want to be a mum.'

Unspoken words were an undercurrent that pulled Cade away from a perspective that felt suddenly selfish. He needed to know what it was that he could feel but didn't understand.

'It means a lot to you, doesn't it?'

'So much.' She pressed her fingers against her lips for a moment. 'Too much maybe. Which might be why I kept putting off making a decision. What if…' The vulnerability in Jo's eyes was far more heartbreaking than any broken words. 'What if I fail at being a parent?'

Cade was genuinely astonished. This clever, courageous, compassionate woman doubted her ability to raise a child? 'How could you possibly do that?'

'I'm sure almost every parent does their best, but it doesn't always work out, does it? Sometimes…sometimes that child grows up to believe they're not good enough. Perhaps, deep down, they believe that they don't deserve to be loved.'

Wow… How had Cade not realised what had been buried so deeply in Jo's heart? She'd practically spelled it out the first time they'd really talked.

I was such a disappointment to my mother... Unless I did something at least as well as, preferably better than, my brothers, my dad didn't even notice I existed...

Had he missed the significance of what seemed like something to joke about, because Jo herself had never realised how much it had affected her?

'You want to be the parent you never had,' he said softly. 'To get the kind of unconditional love that every child deserves to get.'

Jo was holding his gaze so he could see how his words touched a chord. It was her smile that was wobbly this time, as she broke that eye contact. 'I've got so much love bottled up inside me,' she whispered. 'But I've only just realised how much I need to give it to someone. And babies need lots of love.'

'They do...' Cade's voice was also a whisper.

'We all do, really, don't we?' Jo was staring at her hands. 'Okay, we can learn to live without it if we have to but we know, deep down, that it's the thing we'd choose above everything else if we could.'

'Yeah...' The word was a sigh. 'You're not wrong. I can remember what it was like waiting for my kid to be born. How much I loved her before I'd even seen her as anything more than a blob on an ultrasound screen. Imagining what life was going to be like watching her grow up. We had a name all picked out. Aroha. Love…'

'No wonder you were avoiding me after what I said. That was what made it so hard at the accident today, wasn't it? Why you blamed me?'

Cade shook his head but then blew out a breath. 'I guess I'd been thinking more about the past because I couldn't help thinking about what it would be like to have a baby with you. And that made me think about what my kid might have been like. She'd be nearly ten years old now.'

Jo had her hand pressed against her mouth again, this time to stifle her gasp. 'The same age as that boy who nearly died today.'

'Yeah…' Cade had to swallow a rather large lump in his throat. 'It's not the first time it's happened. In the early days I'd see other people's babies and wonder if she'd smile like that or be falling over when she was learning to walk. I'd see little kids going off to school or I'd go to someone who'd broken their arm in the playground or something and it would cross my mind that she'd be about the same age by now but, you know, I got good at dealing with it. I thought I had it pegged. Until today. But I didn't and it was so hard to make sure it didn't affect how well I could do my job. The last straw was knowing that you could see right through any shield I thought I had and that made me feel more vulnerable than I think I ever have. So I attacked as a form of defence and you caught the flak and I'm really sorry.'

Jo covered his hands, which were making fists on the table, with her own. 'It's okay, Cade,' she said softly. 'Forget it. If it's any comfort, it didn't affect how professional you were at all. I'd work with you any time. I'm really sorry too. For saying something so stupid in the first place.'

'But that's the thing. What you said isn't that stupid. Yeah, I was kind of avoiding you but it was ticking along in my mind somewhere and after today, when I'd calmed down, I knew that it could actually work. For both of us.'

And now, after learning something that he suspected nobody else had ever known about Joanna Bishop—that she'd never known the kind of love that she so very much deserved to have—he was even more convinced that this was the right thing to do. It could be a priceless gift for them both.

'What…?' Jo's gaze was fixed on his face. She didn't understand.

'I'm not saying I could be a real father— any more than I could fall in love with anyone again.' Cade's head shake underlined his words. 'That part of me is broken. But… If anything, today's shown me how haunted I still am by the "what ifs". Maybe being a father from a distance would give me what would fill that hole in my life. I wouldn't have to wonder what my child would be like or what he or she would be doing at any age because I'd know. We'd keep in touch, wouldn't we? They'd know who their biological father was?'

'Absolutely,' Jo whispered.

'And… I really do think you're an amazing person. And I can't imagine how lucky your child is going to be to get all that love you've been saving up for far too long. On the other hand, I *can* imagine what a kid with a combination of our genes might turn out like. How awesome would they be?'

Jo was smiling but it was wobbly. 'They'd end up ruling the world.'

'They'd end up pretty special, that's for sure. Maybe the world needs someone like that.'

Cade could see the way Jo pulled in a very

deep breath. 'This isn't something that either of us should rush into,' she said slowly. 'Especially you, after an overwhelming day.'

'Maybe I needed to get pushed that far. To see things I've been avoiding for ever. To find a more positive way to move on with my life. I've been stuck. I found something that seemed to work but I was hiding, wasn't I? I've been hiding for years and years.'

'So it won't hurt to hide a little bit longer, will it?' Jo squeezed his hands. 'Why don't we get to know each other better? Talk about it more. A whole lot more because there'll be a million things that need thinking about. Give it a month and then you can decide. Either way, I'll be ready to go back to the clinic by then. This is something I know I have to do. And thank you… You've made me feel like it's something I might even be good at doing.'

Cade had long since relaxed the fists his hands had made. He'd turned them over with that last squeeze of hers so that Jo's hands were lying on top of his and he found himself stroking the top of her hands with his thumbs. He was holding her gaze too, and they'd slipped so easily back into that silent kind of communication.

He'd never told anyone his story before

because that had been part of his self-protection. But Jo had seen what was happening, even if she didn't understand why, and she'd cared enough to want to help. She'd listened to every word he'd said and it felt as if she understood everything now. That she knew him better than anyone else in his life.

And after hearing an admission about never feeling loved, that Jo hadn't even realised she was making, it felt as if Cade knew more about her than possibly anyone else in *her* life. They were complete opposites in a way, because he had lost the ability to give love and Jo had too much of it that she desperately needed to give, but that kind of made them opposite sides of the same coin, didn't it? Whatever the analogy, he'd never felt closer to another human being.

He'd never wanted to be this close to someone again. Or to be even closer...? Not simply for the sex, but for the human touch. The connection. Feeling that someone genuinely understood something as visceral as the inability to love and could accept that about him. That they *cared*...

Somehow that silent communication had brought them both to their feet. Into each other's arms. Into a kiss that was erasing every bit of the tension that had been accumulating since they'd last been together like this.

'Come upstairs?' Jo's invitation was whispered when they finally broke the kiss.

Cade's lips were against her neck. 'The only thing I thought to bring was food. Do you have any condoms?'

Jo's huff of breath was a soft laugh. 'Do you know the odds of someone my age getting pregnant naturally? Almost non-existent, that's what. And I'm squeaky clean as far as anything else you might need protection from.'

Cade knew he was also safe and, if the odds of an unplanned pregnancy weren't almost non-existent, it didn't really matter, did it? Not when Cade was quite confident he wouldn't be changing his mind in a month's time.

And what better way to put things right? He could not only wipe out the tension of the last week and particularly today with the kind of communication they could share by making love, it could be like a new beginning as well. A foundation for a future that they might not be going to share in a traditional sense but it could very well be life-changing for both of them. That priceless gift of bringing a baby into the world might be a single thing but it could be given and received by both of them.

He took Jo's hand as they went upstairs.

Whoever had said there was no such thing as magic was definitely wrong.

CHAPTER SEVEN

THIS WAS COMPLETELY NEW.

Totally different.

And so much more exciting than any-thing—or anyone—that Jo Bishop had ever invited into her life before.

Had she had things the wrong way around, all along?

She'd always tried to find that perfect re-lationship—the one that could offer a future that would ensure she didn't miss out on any of the best things life had to offer—only to find they always trailed into dead ends or imploded into messy, hopefully never-to-be-repeated emotional disasters.

This time, she'd defined the future that she knew she wanted and had somehow stumbled into a perfect—for now, anyway—relationship. She and Cade were dating. Ex-cept they weren't because she would have never considered dating someone who was so much younger than her he was almost in a different generation. For heaven's sake, by the time Cade reached his fortieth birthday, she would almost be *fifty*.

No. This definitely *wasn't* dating. They were simply getting to know each other better. It just *felt* like dating. The kind of no-holds-barred dating that you might expect in a couple who'd fallen so madly in love with each other they were going to be married within weeks. Over-the-top dating in a way, because they were taking turns to choose where they went and what they did whenever they had any time off that coincided. There were interesting restaurants from all sorts of cuisines to try and so many places that Jo had never explored. Being mid-spring was a bonus. There were days of perfect weather, there were rhododendron and magnolia trees in full, glorious bloom and Cade, in particular, had a talent for choosing outings that were mini adventures, like that trip to Tunnel Beach had been.

There were echoes of those first hours together in more than the sense of new discovery and adventure. Jo could feel echoes of that urgency to learn as much as possible about Cade in the shortest amount of time. Because it still felt as if this could be what had been missing from her life? If so, Cade seemed to feel the same way.

This was different, however, because they both knew there was no possibility of a long-term relationship, let alone the prospect of getting married. Not in the near future. Not ever. And that was fine with both of them. Better than fine, because it provided a safe space in which they could both be completely honest with each other. There was also a perfectly legitimate reason to find out as much as possible about each other, despite the fact they had no intention of spending the rest of their lives together, because they were planning something just as important. Maybe even more important. They were planning to create a new human being that would be a mixture of their genes.

There was so much to talk about. They asked each other endless questions and talked about anything and everything. A lot of it was fun, like comparing likes and dislikes and personality quirks. Some of it was serious, like listing childhood illnesses and family history of any serious health concerns and some of it was difficult to talk about because it was very personal but it was also very necessary—like laying down ground rules. That was probably the most significant conversation that Jo and Cade shared and it happened on the first 'date' after Cade had opened up to Jo about his past. They were in the rhododendron dell on the hilly outskirts of Dunedin's botanical gardens. The scent of the gorgeous flowers, the warmth of a sunny afternoon and a private patch of grass to sit on together made for the perfect setting for perhaps the biggest question.

'How will it work?'

'You probably know more about that than I do.' One of Cade's eyebrows lifted. 'I'm guessing you make arrangements with the fertility clinic and then give me an appointment where I can rock up and...' his smile was cheeky '...make my contribution.'

'I didn't mean the mechanics of being a sperm donor. I meant...you know...later. You said you wanted to stay in touch. Do you want photos? Videos? Real contact—like spending time with him or her?'

Cade's smile had faded completely while Jo was speaking. She saw the way his eyes darkened and the tiny lines at their corners deepened. The movement of his head was a slow single shake.

'Not contact,' he said quietly. 'That's more than I would want. Too...close.'

Jo understood. He didn't want to get close

enough for his child to steal his heart. To present a risk of the new life he had so carefully built for himself falling apart because of another overwhelming loss.

'But you'd like them to know who their biological father is?'

'When it's time. Aren't there laws around adoption and, presumably, sperm or egg donation that mean someone can trace their biological parents when they're eighteen?'

'I think so. But there's also DNA tracing now, which changes things. It's possible your child could turn up on your doorstep one day, with no warning. Would you be able to cope with that?'

'They'd be an adult. It feels like that would be very different to meeting a kid.' Cade closed his eyes for a long moment. 'Yeah...' he said, finally. 'I reckon I can cope with that.' He opened his eyes to meet Jo's gaze. 'But what will you tell them when they're young? When they start asking questions about why they don't have a daddy like other kids?'

'Traditional nuclear families are only one variety these days. Single parents, blended families, same-sex parents... Different is so normal I don't think they'll be anything more than curious—about who you are, not so much why you're not in their life.'

'What will you say?'

One of the large, pale purple blooms of the closest tree gave up holding onto an over-laden branch. It separated into single trumpets that settled on the grass between Cade and Jo. She picked one up, bringing it close to her nose to inhale the gentle scent.

'I'll say that their daddy was a very special friend who couldn't have his own family but really wanted to help me have someone to love *this* much…'

There was a moment's silence. Jo could almost hear Cade swallowing hard. She certainly heard him clear his throat.

'He'll ask "why?" Or she will.' Cade also picked a trumpet. He touched the darker, speckled part of the flower at its centre. 'I hope it's a girl. I'd like her to grow up to be as awesome as her mum.'

It was Jo's turn to swallow hard and clear the prickle behind her eyes. If only things were different, Cade would be exactly the person she would choose to not only father her child but to *be* their father. Her partner. Because he was the first person in her life who made her almost believe she *was* awesome when it had nothing to do with her professional skills. That she was special enough to deserve the kind of love she'd never been given.

But things weren't different and, in many ways, it was going to make this all a lot easier. She would be able to focus completely on being the best single mum possible, which would be quite enough to juggle along with her career. How much more complicated would it be to be trying to be the best lover or partner or wife at the same time?

'I'll tell her that you couldn't have a family because you're a hero. That you have to go to all sorts of dangerous places to save lives.' She offered Cade a smile. 'Like Superman.'

He gave a huff of laughter. 'Might work for a six-year-old but I can just imagine what a teenager would think of that.'

Jo shrugged. 'They'll be smart enough to know that relationships can be impossible for all sorts of reasons.'

'I wouldn't want them to think they were unwanted.'

'They won't. They'll be the most wanted baby ever.'

'I mean by me. I'd like them to know that their existence isn't an accident. That we planned this?'

Jo nodded slowly. 'Let's take photos,' she suggested. 'I'll frame some—in one of those multi-picture frames—and keep them on a wall where they'll be seen every day. They'll grow up to know your name and that you were my friend and when they ask questions about their daddy I'll be completely honest and it will be…' Jo had to pause and take a breath. 'Just the way things are, I guess. You will always have been part of their life in a way.'

'And when they ask where I am?'

'I'll probably be able to be completely honest about that as well and say I have no idea.' She dropped the now bruised petals in her hand. 'You will have long moved on by then. You could be anywhere in the world.'

There was a longer silence this time. Cade was clearly thinking about everything she'd said. Jo didn't realise she was holding her breath until she heard Cade release his in what sounded like a sigh of what…relief?

She certainly felt relieved. Cade was happy with the ground rules. They were a big step closer to making this happen.

'So…photos, huh?' Cade pulled his phone from his pocket. 'Somewhere where they're seen every day? We'd better make them good.' He wriggled closer to Jo and held the phone above them. 'Do you know, I've never taken a selfie?'

'Me neither.' Jo could see her face, and Cade's, on the screen of his phone. He was making a silly face and she was laughing as she heard the click of the first image being taken.

This was new.

Not completely new, because there were echoes of what he and Nina had found together all those years ago. Like the closeness that came with being able to be absolutely honest with another person—about absolutely everything, including things that had been hidden from anyone else in his life— even from his family because he didn't want them to be worried about him. It was cathartic to admit weird things, like that early habit of compulsively searching crowded places, in case there was a baby or child of about the right age and hopefully skin colour that gave him a moment of thinking…yes…that could have been my child. That could have been what my life would have looked like. Maybe it had been a version of poking at a wound to see if it was healing and when the need to poke had lessened and it only happened by accident he knew he was dealing with his loss. That he could live with what was missing.

He'd forgotten about the excitement of being able to share dreams for the future with someone else, though.

Not the same future exactly, of course, and that was what made it safe enough to enjoy that excitement and to take pleasure in being part of its creation. Cade would move on—sooner or later—to live the same life he'd been living for the last decade but he would take with him the satisfaction of knowing he had helped a remarkable woman achieve her dream of motherhood. He would have filled the gap in his life that had haunted him by being able to watch—to care, maybe to worry but no doubt also feel very proud—from a distance, as his child grew up. There was something rather nice about knowing that he would be part of the small person who would have Jo's total love, guidance and protection on their journey to adulthood. He would never be *too* close to either of them, however, and that way there was no threat to limiting where he went with the career he loved and the risk to his heart was perfectly manageable.

There was also something more than nice about knowing that his photo would be on the wall of the house they lived in. That he would be seen as a real person and that his child would know that he had been wanted by both his parents. To that end, Cade had put some effort into learning how to take a good selfie, but today's setting, about three weeks into the month they had allocated to get to know each other properly, was providing a distinct challenge.

They were on an exposed part of the Otago Peninsula's coastline, on a viewing platform that gave them a spectacular vantage point to watch the flight path of members of the royal northern albatross colony as they came into their only mainland breeding area in the world. The fierce wind, which helped chicks learn to fly later in the season, was not only uncomfortably cold—it was playing havoc with their hair as Cade tried to take a photograph with the lighthouse at the head of the peninsula just visible in the distance behind them and hopefully also with one of the magnificent seabirds showing off its three-metre wingspan.

'That's no good, you're missing an eye,' Cade told her as he checked the image. 'And my hair's starting to look like one of the nests those big birds are building.' He held the phone up to try again. 'Reckon it might be time to cut it off.'

'*No...*' Jo was laughing as she pulled her hair behind her ears and the wind instantly whipped it out again. 'Your hair is one of the things I love most about you.'

The wind, in combination with the laughter, seemed to swallow most of her words. The ones that he could hear the most clearly sounded like 'I love you...'

It should have been enough to sound the kind of alarm that had always signalled the end of any past relationship Cade had included in his life but...this was different, wasn't it? There was an agreed plan in place and a limited time that they were going to be together like this. They were getting to know each other and they were almost through the month that Jo had stipulated they needed before making a final agreement. He had no trouble putting a smile on his face as he tapped the screen to take a rapid volley of shots. Surely one of them would be a much better photo for that frame.

They re-joined their tour guide to hear about the breeding cycle of the albatross and see the nest building that was being done by the male birds and the courtship dances that were happening nearby.

'That's called a "sky-point",' the guide told them, 'when they lower the head and then swing their beak up sharply like that. And that's "sky-calling". They're showing off their wingspan by extending them and they throw in a "sky-point" and the loudest call they can make for good measure. Never fails to impress the girls.'

The noise was raucous. The wind was cold and, for most women, it would probably have presented a date from hell but Jo was clearly loving it. She was grinning at Cade as the guide was speaking. And then she elbowed him in his ribs as they moved on.

'I wouldn't advise it,' she told him. 'For any girls you might want to impress in the future.'

'Noted,' he said. But impressing unknown females in his future was the last thing on Cade's mind. He couldn't—or didn't want to—begin to imagine it. How on earth was he ever going to find someone that he enjoyed being with as much as Joanna Bishop?

He didn't want to think about it but he couldn't shake it out of his head when they were walking back to the car park. This month of being together as much as possible was going too fast. What would happen next? Would the plug be pulled straight away from their time of having adventures together like this? They'd been to every beach they could find within a reasonable travelling time, checked out museums and public gardens, the heritage attractions and art in the harbour settlement of Port Chalmers and enjoyed a performance by the city's champion bagpipe band in the Octagon, in the shadow of Robbie Burns' statue.

Would the interesting taste-fest of sharing meals at an eclectic variety of restaurants also have to stop? Okay, they'd probably tried most of the best already but he would be quite happy to go back to a lot of them and eat the same food. Like the Viking style sardines at a very cool Nordic gallery/restaurant combination and the best fried chicken he'd ever had at the Southern USA style eatery in the central city. They'd sampled Italian food, Asian fusion, Hungarian and there was always that amazing hamburger joint to go back to, along with the deli that was Jo's go-to for a meal at home.

And what about the best sex Cade had ever experienced? That probably had to stop even before Jo got pregnant. How quickly would that happen? And *then* what would happen? Would she want him to be involved with the birth? Did *he* want to be involved?

And, if he didn't, where in the world would he go next? He didn't want to think about that either. Because, right now, he didn't want to *be* anywhere else in the world.

Cade had pulled out the big guns with it being his turn to organise this time together. Jo wasn't due to start her next shift until tomorrow afternoon and he was doing a night shift so he'd added a surprise on to the visit to the albatross colony.

'We're not going home,' he told Jo as he handed her a helmet to put on before they got back on his bike.

'What? Never…?' Jo's eyes were dancing.

'Not till tomorrow morning. After a sleep in. In a castle. New Zealand's *only* castle, no less.'

'Oh… I've heard about the castle. That's somewhere else I've never been.'

Cade jammed his helmet over his wayward and now probably tangled waves. 'Excellent. First times are always the best.'

That wasn't entirely true, Jo decided later that night.

Part of it was. Not knowing what to expect from visiting an albatross colony or exploring the wonderful castle and its gardens that was another popular landmark on the Otago

Peninsula made a first time something extraordinary, it had to be admitted. But *this*… this feeling of lying in Cade's arms after they'd made love was getting better every time it happened and Jo had lost count of how many times that was now. Getting to know exactly what could take their intimacy to the next level, tease an arousal to new heights and deliver a climax that could leave them both beyond satisfied hadn't actually been a consideration when Jo had suggested getting to know each other well enough to make a well-considered choice about something as big as Cade becoming the father of her baby, but…wow…it was a bonus that she would remember for the rest of her life.

They were in a luxurious room in a lodge built on the seaward side of Larnach Castle, beside the historic stables. The brass bed ends were antique, the soft, warm duvet and pillows made the bed a nest that Jo had no intention of getting out of any time soon and, through the windows, she could see the stars of a clear night sky. She could hear the steady breathing from Cade, who was still holding her in his arms but had clearly slipped into sleep, and she could smell the scent of him—of *them*—and…she had never felt quite this contented and happy. Ever.

Jo shifted just a little. Enough so that she could touch Cade's skin with her lips and taste him as well as be aware of his scent. She shifted her hand carefully too, spreading her fingers so that every fingertip could feel a separate patch of skin on his chest that included smooth skin, chest hair and a disc of a nipple that was hardening instantly despite a touch that was no more than the kiss of a feather. Tilting her head, Jo could see that Cade was not asleep, after all. He was watching her with those gorgeous dark eyes, the strong lines of his face softened by the waves of his hair and a smile on his lips that was so tender it broke her heart.

Dear Lord, she loved his face.

She loved *this*—being naked in his arms and feeling his skin against hers.

How could Cade really believe that he wasn't capable of being in love with anyone again? That that part of him was broken beyond repair? Jo could see it there—his ability to love—so close to the surface in that smile and the look in his eyes. She could feel it, even, with just the memory of how his touch could make her feel.

But Cade wasn't aware of it. And if he had been Jo knew he would not be here with her like this. He wouldn't have offered to be a part of helping her achieve her dream of becoming a mother, and she was beyond grateful for that. She could also be grateful that the sex had been the perfect end to a perfect day and it was going to be pure bliss to drift into sleep knowing that neither of them needed to set an alarm to rush into work early in the morning.

She was going to miss having these adventures with her cowboy Cade when he moved on. No…she was going to miss *him*. In that split second, as her own lips curved in response to that smile on his face, Jo realised just how much she was going to miss him because it wasn't just this man's face or his lovemaking or his company in having adventures that she loved.

It was him.

And it wasn't just that she loved him in the way you could love a good friend. It felt as if she was *in* love with Cade. Jo found herself closing her eyes as the disturbing thought filled both her mind and her heart. So that Cade couldn't see it as he dipped his head to kiss her again. She did her best to dismiss it and, thankfully, that became so much easier as his lips touched hers and desire was rekindled.

Falling in love was not part of any plan

to get to know each other better. There was a tacit agreement between them that it was forbidden, in fact, so it couldn't be allowed to happen.

Because it could change everything.

Maybe it already had…

CHAPTER EIGHT

CPAP.

Continuous Positive Airway Pressure.

A ventilation technique that could be beneficial in all sorts of clinical situations, like heart failure, chronic obstructive pulmonary disease, pneumonia, chest trauma including a flail segment, toxic inhalations of chemicals or smoke, obese patients, near drownings... the list could go on.

It should go on but Cade found himself simply staring at the screen of his laptop, his mind drifting away from this presentation he was supposed to be working on. His abstract and outline had been accepted for the programme of an international emergency medical conference next year in Europe. Prague, no less, which was a city he'd never been to. It could be where fate intended him to go next, given that he'd just received the final acceptance of his proposal to join what would be a very well-respected gathering of experts in pre-hospital medicine and the fact that the timing could be perfect. It might be better if he was gone from Dunedin well before Jo had her baby. Before it was obvious she was pregnant, even?

Except…something seemed to have changed, although Cade couldn't quite put his finger on what it was. Perhaps it was actually because nothing had changed? The end of the month deadline for confirming his decision had come and gone and he'd made it very clear he hadn't changed his mind about being a sperm donor for Jo, but nothing much had happened since to move things forward.

She'd been in touch with the fertility clinic in Auckland who had performed the egg collection and freezing process years ago and discovered that they were associated with another clinic in Dunedin so Jo could apparently have any further treatment without the need to travel. The first step would simply be an examination by blood test to check her hormone levels and an ultrasound to make sure no abnormalities had developed in her uterus since it was last checked, but Cade didn't know if that appointment had happened yet, or if it was even scheduled. He had no idea what the timeline might be for moving forward either, and that seemed odd because he knew how important this was to Jo and she had been very aware that time was running out, so surely the sooner they started, the better?

She was working an afternoon shift today so wouldn't be home until nearly midnight, but it was such a familiar action now to pick up his phone and drop a text message that it was becoming automatic. They texted each other at least a couple of times a day and more often if their schedules prevented them from spending any time together, as was happening this week.

Hey...how's your shift going?

Just sending a message into the ether was enough to made Cade feel as if he'd picked up the end of the thread that connected him to Jo. He wasn't so alone in his apartment now and he could flick his focus back to the task at hand. He started reading over the introduction to his presentation.

Single use disposable CPAP devices have become readily available, afford-

able tools that provide one of the most effective interventions in out-of-hospital treatment to assist respiratory effort and oxygenation in patients with acute exacerbation of a wide spectrum of cardiovascular or respiratory conditions.

Cade copied and pasted the list of conditions and situations he'd just compiled and then made a note with a question mark to flag that its inclusion needed more thought.

Evidence from recent studies raises the question of whether it is now a failure in duty of care for any emergency medical service to not have these devices available for every skill level and their use a part of their standard operating procedures: SOPs.

The beep of his phone pulled Cade instantly away from his note.

So far so good. Just had three guys in who had a bit of a disagreement at the pub. Total of fourteen stab wounds to assess.

OMG. Sounds messy.

Mostly superficial. One deeper wound that reached a kidney but no surgery advised. Lots of stitching up lacs. Gave Security a bit of fun keeping a lid on things.

Cade was frowning. The thought of Jo being anywhere near drunk, violent men angered him to the point where he had to unclench a fist to respond to the message.

Be careful.

Will do.

She added a thumbs-up emoji.

Still on for tomorrow?

Cade had said he wanted to come and watch one of her fencing classes. Maybe even give the sport a go himself.

En garde! came the response.

Who knew there was an emoji of someone with a sword and a mesh mask?

Cade put his phone down and turned to his laptop screen again but he found himself unable to focus on what he'd just written. What had become a normal kind of conversation with Jo didn't sound normal any longer, did it? What was going on? He picked up his phone again.

Any word? On a start date?

It took a while for his phone to beep again. No doubt Jo had another patient to see. Or was she avoiding the subject?

No. When Cade was finally thinking about his presentation again, another message came through.

Have spoken to clinic. Will fill you in tomorrow.

It was Cade's turn to send a thumbs-up. He couldn't push for any more information and…it was a start, of sorts, at least. Had the clinic given Jo the green light? And, if so, what was being planned?

The diagram on his screen that he was designing to help explain how CPAP could push fluid back out of the lungs and into the bloodstream by changing alveolar/hydrostatic pressure dynamics failed to recapture his immediate interest. Instead, Cade opened a new browsing window and looked up assisted reproduction clinics in both Auckland and Dunedin. There were different tabs to open that offered all the information he didn't want to push Jo to provide. He sat back and clicked what was a very user-friendly web page. He went to the treatment tab and then chose a sub tab for freezing—sperm, eggs and embryos.

He skimmed over statistics on the age-related decline in fertility and the reasons why women might choose to have eggs frozen, to discover that it seemed a straightforward process to use the eggs. They could be thawed, after an indefinite storage period, by quickly warming them to thirty-seven degrees Celsius. When the cryoprotective liquid was removed and they'd had a bit of time to recover, they could then be injected with a single sperm and the formation of an embryo would be monitored in a laboratory before implantation, usually at an extended blastocyst stage at day five. A pregnancy blood test would be performed nine days later.

Cade's interest was well and truly caught now. He'd had no idea of how advanced technology had become in assisted reproduction. A special IVF culture had been developed, containing a growth factor that occurs naturally in the uterus, to provide better embryo development and chances for a successful implantation. Embryos could be frozen and used later if another attempt was needed— even embryos that had been created from a previously frozen egg. That made it possible to take a biopsy from the embryo's outer cells, freeze it while the cells were analysed for any chromosomal or genetic abnormalities and then thaw and implant it when the results were in.

Would Jo want to do that? Cade went searching again to look for more personal information and found a forum where women could ask questions and support each other through the process. He found a lot of advice that ranged from taking prenatal vitamins to avoiding using plastic water bottles because of BPAs. There were strict guidelines about avoiding salt, caffeine and red meat before a transfer, perfume and stress during and sex or hot baths afterwards. There were superstitions that might seem silly but following them had become like a talisman for good luck. And there was one in particular that made Cade smile.

He'd have to tell Jo about it, he decided, in case she wasn't reading this kind of stuff online. No…he could do better than that. He scribbled a note onto a scrap of paper. He'd

go shopping tomorrow, after work. Before
he met Jo at the fencing studio.

It was getting worse.

That spiral of sensation that Jo could feel,
deep in her belly, when she merely caught a
glimpse of Cade Cameron. It was more than
the stirring of physical desire because it created a warmth that rippled through her body
and that felt more like…relief? Sheer joy that
she was in this man's company again?

Oh, man…

There was no getting away from the fact
that she'd fallen head over heels in love with
Cade.

And it was doing her head in.

He couldn't see her. Or, rather, he wouldn't
be able to tell which of the club members,
paired off and practising techniques, was her
because they were all wearing their protective gear. The jackets and breeches, the steel
mesh masks and Kevlar neck bibs, the glove
on the sword hand, the chest protector.

Jo could see Cade, though. He was talking to the head instructor, who seemed to
be explaining the positions and moves that
people were making and the footwork they
were using. Feints and parries, ripostes and
lunges. Jo wanted to improve her footwork

to enable her to better control the distance between herself and an opponent as she stayed within the limits of the allowed width of the 'strip'. The fact that she was being watched—and that the instructor might have pointed her out to Cade—should have made her able to focus more clearly and do her best to impress him but it was unfortunately having the opposite effect.

She couldn't concentrate well enough because she was so aware of Cade being here. Of how she felt about him and of the growing tension of not only debating whether or not to tell him how she felt but whether she could go ahead with the plan of him being the father of her baby. This was her fault, wasn't it? She'd wanted to know her donor but she'd allowed it to go too far. Too deep. She could keep her feelings secret, of course, and Cade would move on and out of her life, probably before her baby was born. But could she live with carrying and then raising a child that would remind her every day that she'd found the love of her life but it was impossible for them to be together? It wasn't just the age difference. Cade had made it very clear that it was the last thing that he would ever want.

It would be far easier to have a baby and

be aware only of the information that was made available by the sperm bank. To have no personal connection with the father at all.

'Sorry...' Jo shook her head at her partner, one of the more senior members of the club. 'I nearly tripped over myself. Can I try that again?'

'Sure. Try and keep your lead foot pointing forward and your back foot perpendicular. And maybe lean forward a bit more?'

Jo tried. She did better the next time but, if this had been a competition, her partner would be wiping the floor with her. She couldn't help sideways glances towards Cade. Or the track her mind insisted on returning to.

She couldn't pull the plug on the plan simply for her own future peace of mind. Cade wanted this as well. Not as much as she did, perhaps, but it was still important to him. It would allow him to be a father in the only way he could deal with it—from a distance. He couldn't be so involved that it would open old wounds and remind him of the pain of losing the love of *his* life and the baby they'd almost had.

Telling him how she felt might do that too.
She couldn't tell him.
She *had* to tell him. Because this was the

most honest relationship Jo had ever had with anyone. She felt as if she was increasingly living a lie and it didn't sit well at all. Cade deserved better.

'Sorry...' Jo had to apologise again as she failed to put up any kind of defence that her partner had to get through. She was fencing like a complete beginner. 'I must be tired, I think. Or brain dead.'

'No worries. Let's call it quits. Class is nearly over, anyway.'

Jo pulled off her mask as they made their way to the edge of the space. Cade was waiting for her and, because he didn't know anything about fencing, he was looking beyond impressed. She could see admiration and respect in his eyes and something that looked a lot like pride and that was enough to break her heart. He was *proud* of her?

He wouldn't be if he knew the truth.

That she had broken what was probably the most important rule.

'I won't be long.' Jo softened her brusque greeting with a smile. 'I'll just get changed.'

'Take your time,' Cade said. 'I'm loving this. I think I want to sign up.'

'Great...' The instructor slapped him on the back. 'Let me check when we've got a new introductory course starting.'

* * *

They picked up hamburgers and took them back to Jo's place but she really wasn't hungry tonight. The odd glances she was getting from Cade told her that he was aware of the tension, but then it became obvious that he thought he knew what was causing it.

'Was it bad news from the clinic?'

'What do you mean?'

'You said you'd fill me in on what they told you. But I'm getting the feeling that you don't really want to talk about it. Is there something wrong?'

'No…' Jo shook her head. 'I've got an appointment booked for next week for the check-up. If I'm given the all-clear, I'd only have to wait until my next cycle starts to begin treatment.' She tried to sound upbeat— as excited as she wanted to be about this. 'I'd take medication to optimise uterus lining development, have a mid-cycle ultrasound to assess how it's going and then they'll boost hormones, along with making sure I get all the supplements needed to maximise the chances of the treatment being successful.' Was forcing herself to sound positive helping, in a 'fake-it-till-you-make-it' kind of way? 'The embryo gets transferred about six days after starting the progesterone.'

'I've been reading a bit about it,' Cade admitted. 'I was supposed to be working on a presentation I'm giving for a conference in Prague next year, but I fell down a search rabbit hole and discovered all sorts of things I didn't know. They've made some great advances in the field, haven't they? Like the growth factor they put in the culture when the egg is sitting in the dish for fertilisation and development. Sounds like it improves the chances, especially for older women or someone who's had failed IVF cycles or miscarriages previously. I even read all the messages on a support group page. Oh… that reminds me. I've got something for you.'

Cade put his hand in one of the pockets of his leather jacket hanging over the back of the chair and came out with a small parcel.

'What is it?'

'Open it and find out.'

Jo had to look away from the gleam in Cade's eyes. She had the feeling that he got a lot more pleasure out of giving gifts than he would in receiving them himself and that fitted right in with the character of this amazingly generous, caring man. And it only made her love him even more.

She opened the parcel to find a pair of the softest, fuzziest socks she'd ever felt.

'They're a good luck charm,' Cade told her. 'For Implantation Day. Kind of silly, but it was something I read about in the support group. Apparently, there's a principle in Chinese medicine that claims a "cold" uterus is a cause of infertility. Socks keep it warm and make it more likely that the embryo will stick.'

'Oh...' Jo had to look away from the hope she could see in his eyes now. He really wanted this to work, didn't he? For her. And for himself?

'They're great.' She put the socks down on the table beside her. She knew she should say something else but the words were stuck in a huge lump in her throat. Maybe if she ate something it would get rid of it. She picked up one of the oven-baked potato wedges they'd ordered with their hamburgers. Then she looked at the sour cream dip and actually felt a wave of nausea that made her drop the wedge to lie on the plate beside her barely tasted hamburger. By the time she lifted her gaze back to Cade, the silence between them had grown enough to be an elephant in the room.

'What is it, Jo?' Cade asked quietly. 'What's wrong?'

* * *

The last thing Cade had expected to see was Jo's eyes filling with tears. But he'd known there was something wrong, hadn't he? He'd been sensing that for some time. Weeks, even. Ever since one of their best times together, when they'd gone to the albatross colony and stayed the night at Larnach Castle.

What he really hadn't expected was the way it was making him feel. The inescapable evidence that Jo was a very long way from being happy gave him a catch in his chest that was starting to squeeze like a vice around his heart. That quiver in her voice made it even worse.

'I can't do this,' she whispered.

Cade said nothing. He could only wait for the information that would help him understand. Had Jo decided she didn't want the kind of disruption to her career—and her life—that being a single parent would represent? He would have to respect that, given that he would never choose to allow a child, or anyone else, to become the centre of his own universe, but it was surprising how fast his heart was sinking.

'I thought I could,' Jo continued. 'I thought if I just hid it and you didn't know anything about it, I could carry on and I could have your baby and it wouldn't make any difference to how much I loved her.' Her inward breath was a hiccup. 'Or him…'

Cade was genuinely bewildered now. 'What wouldn't make a difference?' he asked slowly.

'Me being in love with you…'

Oh, *no*…

Okay. *This* was the last thing Cade had expected. He'd been so confident that they were on exactly the same page about relationships and commitment. That neither of them was looking for a significant other in their life. That he knew Jo had gone through her life with the appalling belief that she didn't deserve to be truly loved made this so much worse. How could he have let this get this far without seeing this coming?

'I'm sorry.' Jo was courageously holding his gaze. 'I wasn't going to tell you, but it's been getting harder and harder not to be honest with you. Because…well…because of how I feel about you, I guess. I could never deliberately deceive you.'

The tears in Jo's eyes were spilling out now and rolling slowly down her face. That vice around Cade's heart ramped up the pressure to the point of real pain. He reached out to brush a tear away and, without thinking, he found himself getting to his feet and pulling Jo into his arms.

'I'm sorry too,' he said quietly. 'If I was ever capable of falling in love or wanting to be with someone long term, it would be you. But...' he had to close his eyes against the pain he knew he was causing '... I can't and I'm sorry. I never wanted to hurt you.'

'I know. It's okay. This isn't your fault.' She looked up at him and was doing her best to smile even. 'My bad...'

Cade kissed the top of her head. He should let go of Jo. Say nice things about how special she was and how they would always be friends and then get the hell out of here and as far away as possible. As he'd always done when the women in his life had stepped this far over that boundary line. But his arms refused to obey the command to loosen their grip and...he needed another minute or two to soak in the scent of her hair and the feel of her shape against his body. He was going to miss this so much, but it had always had a time limit and he'd known it was rapidly approaching. He'd just assumed it would all stop in conjunction with the treatment that Jo had wanted so much.

'I was so right when I said you'd make the perfect father,' Jo said softly. 'You still would. But I don't think I could live with just a part of you and not all of you, if that makes sense.'

It did. And he wouldn't want to live with contact for the next twenty years or so as their child grew up, with the reminder that would bring that someone had been, albeit unintentionally, hurt. Children were very good at picking up on emotional stuff like that. His kid might have grown up to hate him because he'd hurt their mother. He might have had an angry adult track him down one day just to tell him what a bastard he was.

'I get it,' he murmured. 'And I know we should just pull the plug before this gets any harder for either of us. Tell me to go and I will, I promise. But...' he pressed his lips against her hair again '...oh, God, Jo... I'm going to miss this. Miss *you.*'

She had her head buried against his chest, which muffled her voice. 'Me too...' She looked up again and he'd never seen her look quite this vulnerable. This...sad. 'Maybe we could just have tonight? One last time?'

How on earth could he say no? Not just to put off the separation in their lives that this change signalled. This could be the last gift he could ever give her. A chance to apologise, even, for his contribution to this having happened. He could do his best to use his touch and, later, his words in the aftermath of intimacy to convince her that she really did deserve to be loved.

Sadly, as they had both known all along, it just couldn't be by him.

CHAPTER NINE

UNLESS THEY WERE bringing in an expected, critically ill patient who needed to get into Resus as soon as possible because they were under CPR, perhaps, or about to bleed to death like the man Cade had brought in with the carotid artery injury, it was emergency department protocol for ambulance officers to wait by the central desk with the stretcher for the triage nurse to tell them where to go.

Hanna was on duty again today and she had a welcoming smile as Cade and Geoff brought their first patient in. With it being the first day of a four-days-on, four-days-off cycle it felt like a long time since he'd been in here. Longer than it normally did, that was for sure. The whole of the last week had dragged noticeably, to be honest, and he knew the reason why.

He was missing Jo.

He hadn't seen her since that last night together. The last night they would ever have together, which had, unexpectedly, hit him a lot harder than any friendship he'd had to walk away from before. If he'd seen her at work in the first couple of days it might have made it easier to navigate the new space they were in but their shifts hadn't even overlapped since then, which wasn't unheard of, but this time it seemed as if Dr Bishop had simply vanished and it was becoming concerning considering how upset she'd been that night.

Cade knew that Hanna was the closest friend Jo had but he wasn't sure he should ask her what was going on. Or how much she might know about his relationship with Jo. It had been a bit of a game to make sure nobody would guess what was going on between them when they were together at work. Maybe Jo had kept it a secret on a personal level as well, like he had? When she'd told him about why becoming a mother was so important to her, he'd had the distinct feeling that it was something she'd never shared with anyone else.

He certainly couldn't say anything to Hanna while he had a patient lying on a stretcher beside him, anyway.

'This is Shona Braydon,' he told her.

'Fifty-seven-year-old, Type One diabetic. Her grandchildren have been off school this week with a gastric bug that's apparently doing the rounds. Shona became unwell and started vomiting today and her daughter called an ambulance when she recognised the signs of hypoglycaemia. Shona was sweating, shaky and very confused. We started a glucose infusion fifteen minutes ago but her BGL was still low on our last check. She's also tachycardic and experiencing transient atrial fibrillation.'

Hanna's glance went straight to the cardiac monitor hooked to the end of the stretcher. The rhythm on the screen was still clearly irregular but she had a reassuring smile for his patient.

'Hi, Shona. You poor old thing, catching this latest bug. My name's Hanna and we're going to get you sorted out, okay?'

'Thank you, dear...'

Hanna shifted her gaze to Cade. 'Room Two's free,' she told him. She had another smile for Shona. 'A private room for you,' she said. 'We only do that for our special patients.'

And the ones who needed isolation to avoid infecting others who might be vulnerable enough for a gastric illness to be a serious complication. Having handed over Shona's care to one of the junior doctors on duty, Cade parked the empty stretcher and stopped to help himself to the hand sanitiser on the desk beside Hanna a few minutes later. He'd been wearing gloves and a mask with this latest case so he wasn't worried about having picked up the bug—using the sanitiser was more of an excuse to pause enough to have a good look around at what was happening in the department.

'Looking for someone?' Hanna asked. 'I think I saw your crew partner heading for the loo.'

'Thanks.' Cade rubbed his hands together to spread the gel. 'It's not norovirus or something going around at the moment, is it?' If it was, they'd need to take extra precautions, especially with any calls to rest homes or other institutions.

Hanna shook her head. 'Just a twenty-four-hour thing. Mainly kids getting it. We have had a few staff away, though.'

'Ah…' Cade let his gaze roam the department again. 'Is that why I haven't seen Jo Bishop for a while?' He knew he might be stepping over that private boundary so he thought fast. 'There was a patient I brought in a week or more ago that I was hoping to follow up on.'

Hanna's quick glance made Cade wonder if she knew more than she was letting on. She was Jo's closest friend, after all. Was it presumptuous to think she'd told him things about her life that she wouldn't have told Hanna? Or anyone else?

'She could have had a mild dose last week. She did take a couple of days off, but she said she thought it was a sour cream dip or something that had made her feel sick.'

The thought of Jo being unwell gave Cade a knot in his stomach. If he'd known about that he would have been there. Taking her some chicken soup or just making sure she was looking after herself. But what if it was actually something she would not have wanted him to know about? Like a broken heart? Because she hadn't let on that she wasn't well when Cade had texted her a day or two after the plug had been pulled on their private arrangement. Her response to his query of whether she was okay had simply been All good. With a smiley face to confirm it.

'You'll probably see her today, anyway.' Yeah…there was a gleam in Hanna's gaze that suggested she was aware that he'd had something going on with Jo. 'She's around somewhere. Ah…there she is.'

And there she was, pulling a curtain back into place as she came out of one of the cubicles. She didn't see Cade straight away so he had a moment to observe that she was looking a bit pale. A bit…subdued? Whatever it was, it gave him a kick in the guts to go with that knot of concern in his stomach. When she looked up and spotted him, her smile and nod of acknowledgement chased the impression away. She looked the way she always did at work. Focused, in control and ultimately professional.

It would have been completely convincing to anyone who didn't know her so well. But Cade did know Jo that well and he knew how courageous she was. How well she'd learned to hide any personal disappointments.

A dollop of guilt got mixed in with the other emotions that Cade was keeping a very careful lid on. This was all his fault. He'd been the one to flirt with Jo in the first place, when he'd written his number on her glove and given her 'that' look when he'd said he would be interested in following up on Kayla's treatment for her badly broken leg.

He'd deliberately made a thing about returning her pen with an over-the-top performance that was intended to let her know that whatever might happen between them would stay completely between them, if privacy was an issue for her. He'd wanted her to know that she could trust him. He'd hoped that she would also like him.

And she had. Enough to choose him as a preferred father for the baby she wanted so much. Enough to give him a glimpse into a life that had shaped her determination and success but also undermined her confidence in how amazing a woman she really was. What Jo needed was someone who would love her so much that they would happily spend the rest of their life convincing her of that. If only things were different, he would have been that man.

They weren't different, of course, but that didn't mean that he had to stop caring about her, did it? He ignored the fact that Hanna was watching him as he stepped close enough to where Jo was bringing up some information on a computer screen to speak to her quietly.

'Hanna thinks I'm asking about a patient,' he said. 'But what I'm doing is asking about *you*… She said you'd been sick?'

Jo kept her gaze on the screen as she

clicked tabs to locate and open a digital patient file.

'I'm fine,' she told him.

There was relief to be found in the genuine warmth of the quick sideways glance Cade received. She didn't hate him, anyway...

'I did have a bit of a bug or something,' Jo added. 'But I'm over it now.'

Another heartbeat of eye contact and he found that their ability to communicate silently hadn't vanished due to the new distance between them. Jo was telling him that she was over how she'd felt about him now. Or would be in the very near future.

'I had to cancel an appointment for that check-up,' she added, turning her gaze back to the screen. 'But I've rescheduled it for the end of this week. I've decided it's time to get things moving.'

That was exactly the way he would have expected Jo to deal with a challenge in her life. To find a solution and make it happen. It was even more of a relief than knowing she didn't hate him for having offered to play a part and then agreeing that it would be better for both of them if it never happened. Cade held that eye contact for as long as he could.

'Hasn't put you off, then?' he murmured. 'I'm glad to hear that.'

'It's made me more determined to get on with it, if anything.' Jo threw him a bright smile. Any observer, like Hanna, would surely think there was nothing personal or heavy about their discussion but Jo lowered her voice anyway. 'At least I know that getting to know my donor is not the best idea I've ever had.'

She was taking the blame herself? Absolving him? Cade wasn't sure he deserved that, but this wasn't the time or place to do anything more than they already had to set their new boundaries and make it clear that anything that had happened between them privately was not going to affect a professional relationship. He didn't want to leave their exchange on a negative note but he could see Geoff walking back into the department and towards the stretcher tucked in against the central desk.

'Best of luck.' Cade returned Jo's smile. He even nodded, as though he'd received the update on a patient he had been seeking. 'I'll look forward to news. And…' He was turning away but he caught her gaze for an extra heartbeat. He wanted to say that her idea might not have been the wisest but that getting to know her so well was something he would never regret. There were no words, however, and real life was pulling them apart. Geoff was beginning to look around the department to see where his crew partner had got to. It was time for Cade to take the first step into his new reality—a world where it would be safer—and kinder—if it did not contain Jo Bishop in anything other than a professional role. His words trailed into almost a sigh.

'…and take care.'

The ambience of the private fertility clinic was one of discreet optimism laced with a confidence that inspired hope. There was a beautiful sculpture of a mother and baby in the entranceway and there was no waiting for Jo's appointment to talk to the clinic's senior specialist.

'I've spoken to our colleagues in Auckland,' she told Jo. 'And we've arranged the transfer of your eggs. As I said when we spoke on the phone, all we need to do is make sure we've got all our ducks in a row and we can get started—possibly on your next cycle. Do you know when Day One of your last cycle was?'

'Um…yes…' Jo told her the date.

The doctor hesitated in marking a calendar. 'You're not sure?'

'I'm sure. It was just a bit slow to get started and a bit lighter than usual.'

'We'll see what's going on with your hormone levels. Let's get your blood test done now, and the ultrasound examination, and then we'll talk through the next steps in more detail.'

The phlebotomist was efficient and the procedure of collecting the blood samples completely painless. Jo was given a gown to change into and then shown into a warm, dimly lit room to meet the ultrasound technician and get settled on the bed.

'Have you had a transvaginal ultrasound done before?'

'Yes. Several times. I had eggs collected and frozen a while ago.'

'Great—' the technician beamed '—you'll know all about inserting the probe yourself, then.' She opened a condom package and slipped the protection over the ultrasound probe.

Oh…help. Would she ever be able to see one of those little packets being ripped open without thinking of that first night she'd had in Cade Cameron's bed? In his arms? On their *first* date? Or what about the second, when she hadn't had one available and she'd had unprotected sex for the first time in her life because, right from the start, that extraordinary trust had been there on both sides? Jo pushed the thoughts away. She was not going to lie here thinking about how much she was missing Cade in her life. This was about moving forward. About achieving what it was that had made it okay to get that close to Cade in the first place—bringing a baby into the world. *Her* baby. Her future.

The technician took control of the probe once it was positioned and then she peered at her screen as various shapes and blobs appeared and faded as she searched for recognisable landmarks. She angled her screen as if it was a normal thing to do to make the images clearer, but Jo went very still. She knew the screen was being angled so that she wouldn't see what was on it. Because the technician had seen something of concern?

Oh, God…was she going to find out that there was actually no chance she was ever going to have this baby she wanted so much because there was something wrong with her uterus? Like a visible mass that could turn out to be cancer and mean she needed a total hysterectomy?

'What's wrong?' she asked. 'Can you see something?'

'Nothing's wrong. I just… I might just see if one of the doctors is free.' She removed the probe and turned her screen off. 'Be right back.' Her smile was reassuring. 'It's nothing to worry about, I promise.'

Yeah…right… You didn't rush off in the first moments of an examination to find a medical opinion on what you were seeing unless something was very obviously not right. The carefully calm expression on the specialist's face when she came in to pick up the probe and turn the screen back on was another giveaway. So was the silence. Jo wasn't going to ask again, however. She was too nervous.

The specialist turned the screen so that Jo could see it.

'Is that…? No… It couldn't possibly be…'

'It is.' The specialist was smiling. 'You're pregnant, Jo. About ten weeks, I'd say, but we'll do some measurements and get a more accurate date for you.'

'But…'

'You did say your last period was lighter than usual. What about the one before that?'

'I…don't remember…' Jo was trying to count back through the weeks. Had she actually conceived that night that she'd assured Cade the odds of her getting pregnant at her age were almost non-existent?

It hadn't been a sour cream dip that was a bit off that had made her feel sick that last night she'd had with Cade. It hadn't been the tummy bug that was going around either. And it hadn't been just that she was missing Cade so much that she'd been feeling so tired and flat and not hungry.

Non-existent odds.

And here she was, almost through the first trimester of a pregnancy.

This was amazing. Unbelievable. For the stunned moment before it hit her, Jo had never felt so happy in her life. And then, suddenly, she'd never felt so afraid.

She had just lost control of how this was supposed to happen. She wasn't ready. This new reality was too enormous to take in. Too good to be true? What if…what if her fear that she would fail at being a parent—like her parents had—was justified? It wasn't as if she would ever have Cade by her side again to make her believe, even for a moment, that she was actually awesome. She would have to cope with her entire life completely changing and would be doing it totally alone.

Jo could feel tears gathering and then rolling down the sides of her face. The technician handed her some tissues. The specialist was blinking quite hard herself.

'I've heard of happy stories like this,' she told Jo. 'But I've never had a front row seat before.'

She thought Jo was crying from joy and she was. As terrifying as this was, there was still definitely joy in that mix of the overwhelming flood of emotions but it was all too much to take in, let alone process, just yet. And there was something new making Jo's heart sink too fast to catch.

This would be worse for Cade than the fact that she'd fallen in love with him.

And, like how she felt about him, there was no way she couldn't tell him that he was going to become a father.

He'd had a bad feeling about this ever since he'd got the text from Jo asking if he could come to her place this evening because she needed to talk to him. This wasn't part of Plan B, which was where he stepped back from any involvement in Jo's private life because he needed to protect her from being hurt any more than she already had been.

And, yeah…he needed to protect himself as well. It had been unexpectedly difficult to step back and he'd found himself thinking about Jo far too much. When he ate anything, for example, it would bring back memories of all the different cuisines they'd tried together. If it was something new, he'd be wondering if Jo would like it as much as he did. If he was tempted by an old favourite, like one of those gourmet hamburgers, the memories—like seeing Jo enjoying her meal so much she didn't care that she had to chase droplets of juice before they could run down her chin—were obviously going to be too raw. Cade had given up eating hamburgers.

He didn't go to bed until he was so tired that he knew he would fall asleep the moment his head hit the pillow because, if he lay awake, he would be far too aware of the empty space beside him. He knew he could easily find someone to fill that space for a bit of fun that wasn't going to go anywhere but he didn't have the slightest inclination to flirt with any of the women he was meeting. On the plus side, staying up late made him way more productive. He'd finished that presentation for the conference in Prague next year. He had been planning to give it a final read-through and polish to email it through this evening, actually, so he'd almost sent a message back to Jo to say that it wasn't convenient to go and see her.

Instead, here he was, on her doorstep. With no takeaway food, or wine, or anything else to offer other than his presence. Because he'd had a bad feeling about that message. Jo had been as aware as he had been that the brief conversation in the emergency department the other day had been a farewell. The closing of the door that had provided an entry into each other's private life. Jo wouldn't be opening that door again if she didn't have a very good reason.

It was Friday today. He hadn't forgotten that Jo had told him she had rescheduled her appointment with the fertility clinic. Had she had some bad news? Had she changed her mind about asking for his help as a sperm donor because there was no suitable alternative available? No…that was ridiculous. It was more likely to be that she'd been told she could never carry a child for some reason and perhaps he was the only person she knew would understand how devastating that kind of news would be.

Cade's heart sank even further on seeing Jo's face when she opened the real-life door of her house to invite him in. He'd never seen her look like this. Or to be clearly summoning her courage to say anything. She took him into her living room, which might well have been a conscious choice because they'd never spent time together in here, they'd only used the kitchen and bedroom on his previous visits. This was a lovely room, lined with overstuffed bookshelves and with a gas fire providing the light and heat of real flames.

The silence grew when they were both sitting in old armchairs on either side of the fire.

'Can I get you a drink? Coffee or something?'

'No, I'm good, thanks.' Cade bit his lip, stopping himself from asking Jo what was wrong. What if she burst into tears like she had the last time he'd done that? He'd have to take her in his arms and comfort her and he knew where they'd end up. Exactly where they'd ended up last time. In her bed. That Cade could already feel the pull of wanting to provide that sort of comfort again was a warning he wasn't going to ignore. He was too involved, here. Jo didn't need him. She'd always coped on her own and she'd need to do that again in the very near future. The best thing he could do was to encourage her to do just that.

Or maybe she didn't need his encouragement. She was taking a deep breath. 'I'm sorry to summon you like I did but there's something I have to tell you and I thought it would be better for it to be completely private.'

Cade nodded. He was watching Jo's face but she was looking at the flickering flames of the small fire.

'I had the appointment at the clinic this afternoon,' she said. 'Blood tests and an ultrasound.'

He nodded again. 'That's good news. Did they give you an idea of when you can start treatment?'

'I'm not going to start treatment,' Jo said quietly. 'I can't.'

Cade closed his eyes for a long moment. So he'd been right. Jo had developed an abnormality that would prevent her being able to get pregnant. His heart was breaking for her as he opened his eyes again to find that Jo was the one watching him carefully now.

'I'm pregnant, Cade,' she said.

There was an odd buzzing sound in Cade's ears which was possibly why he'd misheard what Jo had said.

'Sorry…what did you just say?'

She was taking another deliberate breath.

And she spoke slowly and very clearly. 'I'm pregnant. Just over ten weeks.'

The buzzing sound had gone but now there was some kind of mental fog rolling in that made it impossible to do the maths. A gestation was counted from the first day of a woman's last menstrual cycle, wasn't it? Which meant that you had to subtract a couple of weeks to come up with a conception date?

'I'm sorry,' Jo whispered, her gaze sliding away from his. 'I really did believe that the odds of conceiving naturally at my age were almost non-existent but that must have been when it happened. That first night you stayed here with me and I didn't have any condoms in the house.'

'Not your fault,' Cade muttered. 'Everyone has to take accountability for their own protection.' He'd thought about it at the time, hadn't he? He'd dismissed both the likelihood of it happening and that it could be a disaster if it did because, after all, he was planning to father a baby for Jo when he'd gone through the time period she had deemed necessary to be sure. 'It's not as though that was the only time.'

'I had no idea that I was pregnant. I was still getting my period, although it was lighter than normal. I thought that I'd picked up a dose of mild food poisoning from that sour cream dip we'd had that night. I was pretty sure you hadn't eaten any of it, so I didn't say anything at the time.'

Cade finally met Jo's gaze again. 'How do you feel about it?'

'I'm not sure,' she admitted. 'I'm all over the shop, to be honest. Part of me thinks it's some kind of miracle. I'm over the moon but I feel really guilty as well. As if I did it deliberately to someone who had no idea it was a possibility.'

'Well…' Cade managed to find a wry smile. 'That last bit's true.'

'And we'd both agreed that it wouldn't be a good idea to go through with the donor bit, given my feelings for you but…' Jo was holding his gaze and she looked as fierce as he'd ever seen her look '… I can do this. I'm already getting over it. I think we can end up being simply friends. That we can go back to the plan and you can be a father at a distance. That part doesn't have to change at all.'

This time, Cade shook his head. 'But it already has.'

'How? The end result would have been the same, wouldn't it? I'd be pregnant and we wouldn't be spending so much time with each other. You'd be totally free to get on with your life anywhere in the world. It's just happened in a different way. Without a laboratory and procedures to go through. And I'm suddenly a lot further along the track too, I guess, but that's a good thing in a way. The risk of something going wrong in the first trimester would have been scary.'

Cade had stopped taking in her words by the time Jo had finished speaking.

'It is different,' he insisted. 'I was prepared for being part of a medical procedure. A legal agreement, even, but…but we made a baby the normal way. The way…'

Oh, God…the way he and Nina had made *their* baby. By making love.

Shaking his head again wasn't going to help his thoughts fall into a space where he could deal with them. He had to move. He got to his feet without being aware of sending any instructions to his legs.

The expression on Jo's face as she looked up told him that she'd guessed what he'd been thinking. That she knew she had caused him pain by reminding him of what had shattered his life so completely all those years ago. She didn't want to hurt him any more than he'd ever wanted to hurt her.

'It's okay,' he said. 'Or it will be. It's a bit of a shock, that's all. I don't know how I feel about it. I need some time to think.'

Jo was on her feet now. She had her arms wrapped around her body and was she carefully keeping herself out of touching distance from him?

'I know...and I'm sorry. But it wasn't something I could tell you by a text message or phone call. I can keep this as private as you want it to be.'

'Thanks...'

'And it will be okay.' The tilt of Jo's lips was poignant. 'Maybe miracles don't happen unless they're meant to?'

The hope in her eyes almost took his breath away but it was the way Jo's arms loosened to leave her hands resting on her belly that pushed this a bit further than Cade could deal with right now.

'I can see myself out,' he told her. 'We'll talk soon...'

Cade would have no idea that Jo was upstairs, in the darkness of her bedroom, watching him ride away on his bike.

Or that he was taking a good chunk of her heart with him because she understood exactly how he felt right now. Blindsided. Afraid of how this could affect the future. Having memories come at him from all sides to remind him that he'd been right to protect himself from anything like this being able to happen again. She could understand all too well why Cade was so afraid to let love back into his life because this was so, *so* huge.

She wanted to protect him herself but she couldn't change this reality. And she didn't want to change anything now. Again, she found her hand resting on her belly and the gesture had become a kind of touchstone in the last few hours. She had someone else to protect now. She already loved this baby who was safely cocooned in her womb and she knew it was enough to stand up to the fear she'd had herself, that she would fail as a parent.

There was one thing she certainly wouldn't fail in providing. This baby would grow up to know how much it was loved and that it deserved to be loved that much. Cade had understood that she wanted to be the parent she'd never had herself and, while Jo knew it wasn't going to be easy, she also knew that she *could* do this. She had more than enough love to make it work. And Cade had given her more than he realised.

He'd made her believe, on more than one occasion, that she deserved to be loved herself.

That she was, indeed, awesome.

If—or rather when—things got tough, she could hang onto that. As tightly as she needed to. Times like now, in fact, as she had to admit she hadn't been telling the truth when she'd told Cade that she was already getting over being in love with him.

CHAPTER TEN

'CANCEL… CANCEL. STAND BY, PLEASE…'

Cade picked up the dashboard microphone. 'Roger that.' He glanced sideways at his partner, one eyebrow raised. It had to be something major coming through to bump an elderly person who had probably fractured their hip further down the queue.

The radio link to Control crackled back into life. 'Code One… Go to twenty-six Montgomery Crescent, repeat—two-six, Montgomery Crescent. Two-year-old boy found at bottom of swimming pool. Unresponsive.'

Cade swore under his breath, hit the switches to activate the beacons and siren and put his foot down. His sideways glance this time was not to take in the grim expression on Geoff's face but to check that the sat nav was providing directions to the address.

'Next right,' Geoff said. 'And then first left. It's only two blocks away.'

Cade changed the siren sound as they reached the intersection, but he slowed the ambulance for only a few seconds.

'Clear left,' Geoff said.

They could see a woman on the street, frantically waving, as soon as they turned into Montgomery Crescent. Cade turned off the siren but the beacons were still flashing as he backed swiftly down a wide driveway and they grabbed the gear they needed. The bars of the metal pool fence and the wide-open gate made it easy to see exactly where they needed to go. A man was kneeling beside a tiny, still figure. He raised his mouth from the child's face and began pushing on the small chest. His hair and clothes were soaked and dripping. A woman crouched beside him, holding her head in her hands as she made distressed sounds.

'How long?' Cade asked the woman who'd been waiting for them on the road. 'How long was he missing for before he was found?'

'Only a minute.' She looked terrified. 'His dad was cleaning the pool and he just came inside to get a bucket.'

She was following Cade and Geoff as they walked swiftly to the scene. It was tempting to run but they were trained not to. It wasn't simply that they could trip and damage equipment or themselves, rushing into a scene created a frame of mind that was not conducive to dealing effectively with a life-or-death situation.

'He saw Toby as soon as he went back and we saw him dive straight in the pool. He knew to start CPR.'

'That's great.' Cade was beside the boy's father now. 'You're doing a great job. My name's Cade. Let me help you...'

'I'm not sure I'm doing it right...' The boy's father was moving back to let the crew close to his son. He was young, probably only in his late twenties. 'It's a long time since I did that first aid course.'

Any CPR was better than none, but Cade could see the ominous blue colour of cyanosis on the child's lips and fingers and he knew even before he began his assessment that he was going to find him not breathing and probably without a pulse. Geoff was already setting up the defibrillator and had the pouch open to take out the pads he needed to stick on the boy's chest. Cade kept up the CPR until Geoff had applied the pads and then unzipped the backpack he'd carried from the ambulance and took out an airway roll and a bag mask as they paused just long enough to see what was happening on the screen.

The boy's father had his arms around the woman who was still crouched on the ground sobbing.

'You're Toby's mum?' Cade asked gently.

'Y-yes...' It was the man who responded, through chattering teeth. There was enough of a wind to be a concern for anyone who'd been immersed in cold water.

Cade turned to the second woman. 'Could you maybe find some blankets in the house? Geoff will give you a foil sheet to put round Toby's dad as well.'

Geoff nodded acknowledgement of Cade's suggestion but his gaze was fixed on the screen of the monitor. 'Looks like normal sinus rhythm,' he relayed.

Cade put his fingers on the child's neck again but he was already shaking his head. 'There's no pulse,' he said. 'Could be PEA.'

Pulseless electrical activity, where the heart was still receiving signals to contract but there was either no response or it was too weak to be able to generate a pulse or provide circulation. It was also not a shockable rhythm.

'Carry on with compressions,' he told Geoff. 'I'm going to intubate.'

Getting an airway secured was the first priority. Ventilating the toddler to get him breathing again was the next and the most effective way to do that if the lungs were full of water was to have the airway secured with an endotracheal tube. Compressions to keep his blood circulating were just as important and getting IV access for the drugs needed for resuscitation was another priority. The ABCs. Airway, breathing and circulation. The foundation of a first response in any emergency. They had protocols to follow so it was easy to be completely focused. To know exactly what needed to be done and not think of anything else.

'Let's have continuous end-tidal CO_2 monitoring and the pulse oximeter on,' Cade directed.

'Do you want me to call for a back-up crew to assist with transport?'

There was probably already one on the way because it was standard procedure when they might have to transport a patient under CPR but Cade gave a single nod. 'I hope we'll be on the road before they get here,' he said. 'I'll get IV access and then we'll load and go.'

Placing the endotracheal tube and checking it was in the correct place had been simple. Getting IV access in veins that were not only tiny but now completely flattened by no discernible blood pressure was not going to be simple. Or even possible, given the urgency with which they needed to get this small patient to definitive care in an emergency department.

'I'm going to put a needle into a bone in Toby's leg,' he warned the parents, now huddled inside blankets as they watched on in horror. 'It looks awful but he won't feel a thing, I promise. And it means we can give him any medications he needs.'

He had to cut open the leg of the jeans Toby was wearing, extend his leg and paint disinfectant on the skin below his kneecap. With clean gloves on, he used one hand to locate the patella and stabilise the joint. With his other hand, he picked up the insertion device that looked like a small gun, having already loaded the intraosseous needle. He was aiming for the flat side of the tibia, just below the patella. When he felt the needle touch the bone, he pressed the trigger to start drilling, ready to stop the instant he felt the 'pop' of the needle entering the space within the bone. It took only seconds to put the stabilising dressing patch on and attach the extension that gave them a port to run fluid into as part of the resuscitation and a means of getting drugs into circulation at least twice as fast as peripheral intravenous access in a patient with unrecordable blood pressure.

Cade used that port for drug administration a very short time later, whilst they were en route to the hospital and Toby's heart rate dropped to a bradycardia of only forty beats per minute. The adrenaline he injected raised the rate to well over a hundred beats per minute and lifted the blood pressure enough for Cade to be able to feel both a carotid and femoral pulse. It was only then—with the glimmer of hope that this little boy might be one of the lucky few that survived a near-drowning, perhaps even with no neurological damage—that Cade's focus slipped just enough, for just long enough, to feel a shaft of what Toby's parents were going through.

He could feel some of that fear that they were about to lose their precious child. The guilt that they should have been able to protect him and the potential yawning void of not being able to watch him grow up. And, in the split second before he pushed his own feelings aside to focus again on only what he had to do as this boy's emergency medical care provider, Cade realised that he was feeling this so acutely because he was going to become a father himself.

And he couldn't avoid the risk of loss by taking himself away and watching his child grow up from a distance because it was already there. *His* child—his and Jo's—was already in existence and his need to protect it was also already there. Imprinted into his cells, perhaps, because he knew the pain that loss could bring?

Toby was still unconscious as they stopped in the ambulance bay and Geoff expertly backed up to the ledge. Then he jumped out to pull open the back doors of the vehicle. Having called through the critical status of their patient as they were travelling under lights and siren, there was a team waiting for them, headed by Joanna Bishop. Cade knew she'd had warning of what to expect but he also saw how tense the muscles in her face looked. Was this too close for comfort, in the wake of having only just discovered her own pregnancy? Was she over the shock and already in love with the baby she wanted so much? Surely that would make it even harder to deal with a case like this?

She wasn't showing any signs of stress

that others might have noticed, however. She led the team into Resus, where others were waiting for them, including an anaesthetist and a paediatric critical care consultant that Cade recognised, asking rapid questions as they moved.

How long had he been under water?

Was there any evidence of head or neck trauma?

How long had his rhythm been PEA?

How long had he been receiving chest compressions until a palpable pulse was found?

Exactly what drugs and dosages had he received?

What were the current vital signs? SpO2? Fraction of inspired oxygen?

Toby was still being ventilated but he'd lost the dreadful shade of cyanosis on his lips and fingers and Cade noted that his skin felt slightly warm to the touch for the first time as he helped lift the toddler onto the bed. Jo and the other consultants ordered the remaining wet clothes to be removed and his temperature checked again. They wanted an arterial blood gas measurement, a blood glucose level, a nasogastric tube inserted, a urinary catheter and a chest X-ray. They discussed ventilator settings and the heart rhythm and rate as they switched Toby over to the hospital equipment for monitoring.

It was the controlled chaos of an expert team with a lot to do to save a young life. A nurse was with Toby's parents on one side of the room. Toby's father still had a foil sheet and a blanket draped around his shoulders but his mother looked as if she was too scared to cry any more. It was good that they were being allowed to watch everything being done for their son. Nobody asked Cade or Geoff to leave the room and Cade was quietly finishing his paperwork in the corner, listening and watching what was going on at the same time and keeping his fingers crossed that another urgent call would not come their way too soon. He was still there when Jo stepped back to talk to Toby's parents.

'We're going to keep him asleep for a while so that we can watch his breathing and organ function very carefully and make any adjustments needed.'

'How long…?'

'Possibly a few days but we'll know more tomorrow. Some of the blood tests he's having will let us know whether he's suffered a brain injury from lack of oxygen and he'll have other tests in the next few days. He'll be going up to the paediatric intensive care unit from here, as soon as he's stable, and you can stay with him there.'

'Is…?' Toby's mother was clinging to her husband's hand. 'Is he going to make it?'

'He has a lot of things in his favour,' Jo told them. 'You found him quickly and started CPR and the ambulance crew were not only on the scene almost immediately but got him in here fast and he had a spontaneous pulse again by then. The shorter those time frames are, the more we can hope for the best outcome.'

It was time that Cade left. He tore off the copy of his paperwork that he needed to leave to go in the patient file and signalled Geoff, who began rolling the stretcher out of the area. He was caught by Toby's parents as he went past them, though, and he felt their fear hit him again, but there was something else in the blast of their emotion. Hope. And gratitude.

'We can never thank you enough,' Toby's father told him. 'You have no idea how much it means to us…'

Except he did. And, over the man's shoulder, Cade caught Jo's gaze and it was one of *those* moments. She understood the impact that this case would have had on him even if he hadn't just received the shock news that he was going to become a father again himself. It felt like he was successful in letting her know that he was okay. About more than this case. He was ready to accept the responsibility of becoming a father.

Embrace it, even if he might not be capable of the kind of emotional involvement he might have once been able to offer.

It was Jo's idea that they went for a walk the next time their shifts gave them a window of free time that overlapped. After several emotional days, she was ready for a blast of fresh air and suggested that they went back to Tunnel Beach—the place they'd been when it had actually been a first date.

Before Jo had realised the huge age gap they had.

Before she'd scared him away by telling him that he'd make the perfect father for the baby she was planning to have.

Before they'd made an agreement that had changed everything.

The edges of the shock of what had so unexpectedly happened was continuing to wear off and Jo suspected that Cade was getting his head around the news as well. She'd had a feeling that he might be ready to talk about it after she'd seen him in the emergency department when he'd brought in the toddler who'd come so close to drowning. He was certainly happy to accept her invitation to go for the walk but he refused to take Jo on his motorbike. They went in Jo's car, which was a low-slung sporty BMW roadster.

'You're going to need a new car,' was the first thing Cade said as he folded his tall frame to get into the passenger seat. 'This isn't going to be very practical for a baby seat, let alone the pram and everything else you'll be carting everywhere.'

'Mmm...' Jo threw him a deadpan glance. Did he really think she hadn't already thought of that, along with a million other things that could be important? 'Just as well I gave up riding my own bike, isn't it?'

He was silent as they drove away from the central city.

'How's your week been?' Jo asked. 'You've just finished your night shifts, yes?'

'Yep. It's been good. I've been out and about in my time off, getting to know the city a bit better. There are some really lovely suburbs. I love being up on top of the hills, like in Maori Hill with the spectacular views or over in St Clair right by the beach, but I think I love the peninsula best. Have you ever been to Glenfalloch?'

'Don't think so. It sounds like a good Scottish name.'

'It's a woodland garden that's been around for about fifty years. I was told I'd come at the best time of year to see it and it wasn't crowded when I went on a weekday. There's a restaurant as well. They do a lot of weddings there.'

Jo laughed. 'Probably why it's never been on my radar.'

Cade didn't seem amused. 'It's worth seeing,' he said quietly. 'And a great place to wander around when you've got a lot to think about.'

Like the fact that he was well on the way to becoming a father? Jo was more than sympathetic in that Cade was no doubt dealing with traumatic memories of the last time he'd been preparing to become a father but she was the one who would be facing the most change in her life, wasn't she? Cade might well be gone by the time she was due to give birth. Off doing exciting things with a rescue service or on an oil rig or maybe in some war torn, impoverished corner of the globe.

And she was fine with that, she really was.

Jo's confidence in her ability to cope with whatever the future had in store for her was growing each day.

'How's Toby?' The abrupt change in the conversation made Jo blink. 'Have they woken him up properly yet?'

'Yes. He's going to be discharged, in fact. I did message you about the biomarkers of neuronal damage being within acceptable parameters and the results from the electro-encephalogram?'

'You did. Thanks. Caught me at a busy time so I couldn't respond.'

'And you got the one about the MRI yesterday?' Come to think of it, Cade was much less likely to answer text messages promptly than he had before they had ended their 'getting to know each other' period, even though the subjects had only been professional since then.

'I did. That's why I thought they might have woken him up by now.'

'He's a lucky little boy,' Jo said. 'Fifty percent of children who survive after needing CPR at the scene of a drowning go on to have lifelong disabilities.' She took the turning that led to the Tunnel Beach car park and, despite how low slung her car was, she could feel a stiff sea breeze buffeting the vehicle. It was going to be cold outside. And she couldn't read Cade's mood but it was obviously going to be a very different experience to the first time they'd come here, when it had been so easy to talk to each other.

When they'd held hands to scramble down to the beach and wedged themselves into the gap in the rock to shelter from the wind and there'd been laughter and attraction and an inevitability to the way they'd ended up in each other's arms on the same night. She'd already been on the slippery slope to falling in love with Cade back then, hadn't she? If she'd realised that, would she have backed off before anything had happened?

Perhaps she should have but, if she was honest with herself, she probably wouldn't have. The pull had been irresistible and it was still there. But Jo had already accepted that it was just going to be a background hum in her life. It would be easier to ignore it now that she had her pregnancy to focus on and plans for the future to make. It would be even easier in the long term when Cade was too far away to spend time with him like this. To be close enough to have to curb a desire to touch him or to be searching his face to try and read what he was thinking. And she didn't want to forget it, anyway. She wanted to remember how special Cade had made her feel, but maybe that would also be easier when distance and time had softened the intensity of feelings that were still too close to the surface.

'It looks cold out there,' Cade said. 'And that's quite a wind.'

'Maybe we could both do with blowing some cobwebs away?'

Jo pushed the door open and climbed out of the car. It slammed shut behind her as the wind caught it and her hair flicked over her face so she couldn't even see Cade getting out of his side of the car.

'Jo?'

She tried to tuck her hair behind her ears. Cade was right in front of her now.

'I've had a lot of time to think.' He had raised his voice because the wind was snatching his words away. 'And I've changed my mind.'

Jo's breath caught in her throat. What had he changed his mind about? Had he discovered that he was capable of falling in love? That he'd discovered he felt the same way about her as she did about him? It felt as if Jo's whole world was balancing on a cliff top, not unlike the real ones so close to them on this wild bit of coastline.

'I want to be a part of our baby's life,' Cade said. 'I'm not going to go somewhere else. I want to be a *real* father and take the kind of responsibility that a real father should take. I…' He reached out to hold Jo's shoulders as if he was worried she might be about to turn away. 'I want to marry you, Jo.'

The ground didn't feel stable beneath her feet. It was crumbling, sending her over that cliff, and there were rocks to crash on at the bottom.

'Why?' she heard herself ask. 'Because of the baby?'

A line appeared as Cade's brow furrowed. 'Of course.'

'So, if I wasn't pregnant with your child, you *wouldn't* want to marry me?'

The line deepened. Cade was genuinely puzzled, wasn't he? 'You know the answer to that, Jo. You know why…'

Oh… God… What could be worse than bringing up a child who would remind her every day of the man she'd fallen in love with so hard she would never really get over it?

Marrying him, that was what. Living with him. Knowing that he could never, ever feel anything like the way she would always feel.

Knowing that the baby had been worth staying around for but she hadn't been…

She stepped back, away from the touch of his hands on her shoulders.

'No,' she said. And then she said it again with more emphasis. '*No*. Forget it, Cade. That's the worst idea ever. I'm not about to marry a man who doesn't love me.' She wrapped her arms around herself. It was just the icy wind or the salt it carried that was bringing tears to her eyes. 'You're right. It's too cold.' She turned to pull open the door to her car. 'I don't think I want to walk.'

The silence in the car when Cade got back in would have made the prospect of the drive back to the city very unwelcome except for the crooked smile he offered Jo.

'I'm sorry,' he said quietly. 'It *was* a bad idea. I wasn't thinking straight.'

Jo simply nodded and started the engine of her car. How easy was that for Cade? It hadn't even been a remotely genuine consideration, had it?

'But we can still be friends?'

'Sure.' But Jo didn't turn to meet the gaze she could feel on her skin. She was looking straight ahead of her in the direction that she was heading.

This was a curveball and she needed time

to think about how she was going to handle Cade being more of a part of her future than she had expected. Time to deal with what felt like a damaging blow to the confidence she'd managed to gather about facing single parenthood. About really getting over being in love with Cade. Time to pick up the pieces of her soul from the metaphorical rocks she'd found at the bottom of that cliff.

Had she really thought, for even an instant, that Cade had fallen in love with her? Of course she hadn't. Not really...

But, if that was true, why had it hurt so much to land on those rocks?

CHAPTER ELEVEN

IF CADE WASN'T going to provide the distance Jo knew she might need to keep her heart intact and restore her confidence, she would just have to create it herself by establishing boundaries to keep herself as safe as possible.

It didn't seem to be getting any easier, however, as one week and then another slipped by and suddenly she couldn't zip her jeans up over the neat little round bump of her belly. It was a good thing she wore scrubs while she was at work because no one would guess her secret and there was only one person she had needed to tell so far. It had been far too long since she and Hanna had been out for a meal so her best friend was delighted to spend some time with her.

Amazingly, Hanna had made it easy by guessing the big news that Jo wanted to share, possibly because she'd chosen a soda water for her pre-dinner drink and not her usual glass of wine. Hanna had also assumed that Jo had simply thawed her eggs and become pregnant independently and, for now—until she felt safe enough to cope—it was easier not to correct the assumption.

'Why didn't you tell me? I wanted to help you choose the donor.'

'I think you were out of town that week. That trip to Australia? And we've both been so busy. We've hardly seen each other since my birthday.'

'That's true.' Hanna was too distracted to pursue the dateline. 'Was it hard? To choose?'

Jo could, at least, be completely honest about that. 'Not at all. He stood out from anyone else by a country mile.'

'What's he like?'

'Tall. Healthy. High achiever. Adventurous. Ticks all the boxes.'

'What about getting to know him for all those other boxes that didn't show up on the forms?'

'I decided that wasn't a good idea.' This was also true—she was just leaving out the fact that she'd decided it in retrospect. 'Imagine the complications that could create.'

Like falling in love with someone who was unavailable for the kind of relationship that was enough to overcome obstacles and last for ever? Like having him decide that he wanted to be part of his child's life right from the start, as far as parental responsibilities went? She wanted to tell Hanna about the new issues she was facing but…she couldn't. It wouldn't be fair on Cade. As far as she knew, she was the only person who knew about the tragedy of him losing his family. He had trusted her with a glimpse into a life, and past, that he preferred to keep very private and Jo would have respected that kind of trust from anyone.

Neither was it simply that she needed to be confident about the framework she and Cade were in the process of trying to create that would allow him to be more involved in his baby's life but give her a dignified space to get over being in love with him. And it wasn't just that, either. Even if she did get over being in love with him, she would always care about him enough to want to protect him.

It was a combination of all those things but it also went deeper than any of them. He'd given her the most amazing gift by fathering her child and, in doing so, he'd made himself vulnerable. He must have known he was risking his heart by getting close to something that he'd lost before, with devastating effect—his own child—but she could understand that void of wondering what it would be like to be a parent all too well. She'd been only too willing to let him experience that from a safe distance so, even though it was an alarming change, she couldn't—and wouldn't—deny him the chance to be a father.

Hanna was shaking her head sadly, now. 'You didn't even tell me when you were waiting to find out if it had worked.'

'If something's not very likely, sometimes it's better to assume it's not going to work and save disappointment.' Jo was being deliberately vague. 'I'm telling you now that I'm safely through my first trimester but I'd rather other people don't know yet.'

'Really? How long do you think you can keep it a secret?'

'Long enough, I hope. Another month or two, anyway. I can follow protocols and stay well away from X-rays or infections like shingles.'

'And soft cheese. And sushi. You can't eat that stuff any longer.'

Jo laughed. 'There you go. That's one of the reasons I don't want anyone else to know. I know people would mean well but I don't want the whole world to be telling me how I need to live my life. I've waited so long to do this. I want to do it my way. I'm not even going to tell my mother.'

'I get it.' Hanna held her hands up in a gesture of surrender. 'Sorry. I won't say anything else. It's not as though I know anything from personal experience, anyway. Everyone knows I have no interest in babies or pregnancy. I'll make an exception for yours though, Jo. This one's special.'

Jo sighed. 'That's another reason I'm not ready to go public. Can you imagine what the gossip will be like with me getting pregnant at my age?'

Hanna bit her lip. 'That's true. I'm glad you've told me, though. Let me know if I can help. Do you want company when you go for your antenatal appointments? Like your scans? How far along are you?'

'It's all good.' Jo dodged the question of how far along she was already. 'It's hard enough scheduling appointments in my own shifts without factoring in someone else's. And…you know… I like being independent.'

That hadn't stopped her inviting Cade to come to her next scan but that was different. That was for him far more than it was for herself. The courage he was showing in taking this step in his life was huge, given that he'd told Jo how much he'd already loved his first baby when she'd been no more than a blob on an ultrasound screen. He was putting trust in his ability to cope, in the universe to not let history repeat itself and in Jo, that she was going to allow him close enough to make it happen.

She might not have any influence on Cade's strength or what fate might have in store, but she could at least make sure she didn't break the trust he had in her. You didn't do that to people you loved. She knew how hard it had to be for him to take this step. And even though at the moment it felt like he was only doing it out of a sense of responsibility, surely he wouldn't be able to help falling in love with his child once he or she had arrived safely in the world?

He hadn't expected this to be so nerve racking.

It wasn't as though he hadn't been here before, in an ultrasound suite waiting with a pregnant woman to get the first glimpse of his own child. And maybe that was why Cade's heart was beating so fast. Why he was holding himself so rigidly. Because he knew the impact of seeing those tiny limbs.

A miniature heart that was beating. The smudged features of a small face that would suddenly make this developing child a real person who was going to need all the love and protection of loving parents.

Cade didn't want to feel that slam of emotion. He wasn't ready. He knew it was going to come at some level, because he'd felt the stirrings of it for little Toby who wasn't even his own child, but he still needed some form of protection. Until this miracle baby had, at least, entered the world safely and he'd got past the point where his life had crashed and burned last time he'd been in this position. It was difficult, however. Cade found himself standing, his muscles as tense as if they were poised for flight if necessary. He was far enough away from Jo that, if she reached out her hand, she wouldn't be able to touch him and he was keeping his gaze firmly on the shifting shapes on the screen, rather than risk any of the kind of silent communication that eye contact with Jo seemed to spark.

Not that she was looking at him. Jo also had her gaze fixed to the screen, which was understandable. At this stage of her pregnancy it was possible to see details like fingers and toes, perhaps even facial expressions and to possibly discover the gender of the baby, but Cade had found a new safety net. He could focus on what the technician was doing, as she moved cursors and clicked on points to make measurements and screen for any anomalies. He could watch the clinical data that was being collected as the limbs and spine, the brain, kidneys and heart were examined and measurements recorded.

Cade could see that Jo was as tense as he was, by the way the hand he could see at her side was clenched, but he knew the reasons were very different from his own. Jo had no barriers that could prevent her wanting and loving this child as much as every child deserved to be wanted and loved. Her anxiety was all about how healthy her baby was. Cade's heart gave a painful squeeze when he saw her swipe away a tear of relief when the technician told her that, while a doctor would double-check her findings, she was happy with everything she'd seen. There was a wobble in her voice as well.

'Can you tell whether it's a girl or a boy?'

'Are you sure you want to know?'

Cade couldn't avoid catching her glance as Jo turned her head, her eyebrows raised, asking how he felt about it. The muscles in his jaw might be bunched but he managed what he hoped was a smile that threw the decision back to her. He added a shrug for good measure. He didn't care. It was only the health of the baby that mattered.

'Yes,' Jo said. 'I'd like to know, please.'

'It's just a bit early to be a hundred per-cent sure,' the technician said, moving her transducer again over the skin of Jo's now obviously rounded belly. 'But I did get a good look earlier. And…there…that's a good angle too. Those legs can't be hiding any-thing significant, so I'd put good money on Team Pink.'

Oh…*man*…

A girl.

A daughter.

He could hear his own voice in the back of his head from a time when the plan of fa-thering a baby for Jo had been a very differ-ent proposition.

I hope it's a girl. I'd like her to grow up to be as awesome as her mum…

He'd planned to take Jo out to dinner after this appointment. He had some properties shortlisted and wanted to show her the bro-chures and get her opinion. He'd hoped she might come with him to view the houses, es-pecially the lovely old villa he'd found on the peninsula, not far from those woodland gar-dens, with an amazing view of the harbour.

Instead, he found himself fishing the phone he'd put on silent out of his pocket, as if he'd felt it vibrating to signal a call. He was pretending to read a non-existent message as the technician was using soft paper towels to wipe the gel off Jo's skin.

'Sorry,' he said to her. 'But I'm going to have to go. They're desperate for someone to fill a gap on night shift.'

'No worries.' Jo was pulling up the elastic band of her skirt to cover her belly. 'Thanks for coming, Cade. We'll talk soon, yes?'

'Sure thing.' Cade was already heading for the door.

Heading towards an escape that would give him time to settle the chaos in his head. And his heart. Time to pull the remnants of the defence he needed around himself and shore it up so that it could last the distance. He needed distraction. Maybe a blast of wind in his face from taking his bike out on the open road would do the trick. Because freedom could also be safety, couldn't it?

Jo felt the baby move for the first time about a week after that ultrasound appointment. A tiny ripple of sensation in her belly that was earlier than she'd expected but was unmistakably the movement of those miniature limbs.

Her first thought was to share the news with Cade. To call him. Or hope that he would come into the department with a patient so she could tell him face to face. To find a private space and let him put his own hand on her belly, perhaps, in the hope that he would be able to feel it himself?

Her next thought was a panicked U-turn as she imagined his hand on her belly, knowing that he was only touching her to feel the baby. It was bad enough having him show her pictures of houses he was thinking of buying, knowing that he was only staying in the city because of his need to embrace the responsibilities of fatherhood. She was gradually getting used to the idea of having Cade as no more than a friend and co-parent in the future but it was too soon to think she could cope with him touching her and not have her heart break into even more pieces.

It was, however, time to tell people at work. Not that she'd have to scale back her time on duty or anything, but they'd need time to organise a locum to cover her maternity leave. When the extra pager Jo wore on duty buzzed to let her know a call was coming in for an air rescue that required a doctor on board, her first thought then was that she would have to give up the extra risk that this part of her job presented. Maybe she should step back now, in fact.

Even when she picked up the phone to learn that this was an MCI—a multiple casualty incident, with a crash involving a camper van and a group of cyclists in a gorge not far out of the city and that every resource the emergency services had was being mobilised, Jo was still on the point of telling them she would send someone else from the emergency department. But then she heard that there were children involved and she knew she had to go. This would be the last time. She wouldn't put herself or the baby in any danger but she needed to be there. She needed to do whatever she could to help.

The road was unsealed. It was narrow enough to present a huge logistical challenge to get large emergency vehicles like a fire engine close enough to the scene to be able to do their job which, in this case, might involve getting steel cables attached to a camper van that had tipped over the side of the gulley road after trying—and failing—to avoid a collision with a group of cyclists as it rounded a downhill hairpin bend.

There was a family trapped in that camper van with only a rocky outcrop and a tree that was now on a sharp lean acting as an obstacle to it rolling further towards the bottom of the gully and the river, which wasn't a huge distance but could potentially turn a minor injury into something life-threatening. Nobody could get near it until it was stabilised and there was a terrified family trapped inside. It had been Cade who'd scrambled down, at a safe distance, to try and assess the situation and the first impression was not great. A man was in the driving seat, his head tipped back and his eyes closed.

'Hello…can anyone hear me?'

A woman's face appeared around the unconscious driver's body. There was a trickle of blood on her cheek from a cut on her forehead.

'Me… I can hear you. Help…' She gave a strangled sob. 'I'm too scared to try and get out because I can feel the van move. And I think my foot's stuck, anyway… Please… *help…*'

'That's what we're here for, sweetheart. And don't move for the moment. Stay as still as you can. My name's Cade. What's yours?'

'Jules.'

'Okay, Jules. I can't get any closer just

yet but we're working on making it safe to get you all out as quickly as possible. I need you to tell me everything you can for the moment.'

He quickly discovered that the man in the driver's seat was her husband. He was unconscious but breathing and did not appear to be bleeding heavily. Jules thought she might have broken her arm but she was more concerned about the three children who'd been riding in the back. She could just see her two children aged six and four and a toddler of eighteen months who were huddled in a mess of bedding against the back door, amongst the debris of items that had been dislodged as the van had rolled sideways and possibly glass from the smashed back window. With her foot trapped under bent metal, she was distressed that she couldn't get to her children but Cade was actually happy to hear them crying loudly in the background because it meant that they were conscious and breathing.

'Try not to panic, sweetheart,' he told her. 'Keep talking to the kids. Keep them as still as you possibly can. I'm going back up to the road to let everyone know what's going on but I'll be back very, very soon and then

I'm going to stay with you until we get you out, okay?'

He needed to pass on all the information he'd gained to the scene commander from the fire service. He also needed to see what extra resources were needed and bring a kit back down with him. As soon as it was safe, he had to get close enough to the van driver to assess him properly and start treatment before they extricated him.

Geoff was working in the triage area that had been established to assess and treat the cyclists involved in the accident but, luckily, none of them seemed to be seriously injured. There was another ambulance arriving on scene already and he could see the helicopter he'd requested hovering as they came into their landing area, which had to be further up the road, far enough away to not be creating a problem with dust and stones being thrown up from the unsealed road.

For just a split second, Cade was taken back to the first day he'd met Jo, when she'd flown in with the helicopter crew to work with him in that icy river. That first, utterly captivating glimpse of the intelligence and passion he could see in her eyes was something Cade was never going to forget. Pushing the flash of memory aside came with a feeling of relief that those days were over for Jo. There was no way a pregnant woman would be allowed to jump into a helicopter to take part in any dangerous rescue missions. And thank goodness for that...

He skirted a pile of mangled bicycles.

'Any change in the status of patients?' he asked Geoff.

'No. All status three and four, but most of them are going to need transport. We've got fractures, lacerations and one woman with neck pain and paraesthesia in her hands. We're just getting her on a back board and into a collar. She'll be the priority for transport.'

Cade nodded and kept going. He could see the fire chief directing the deployment of cables and other officers were setting up cutting gear that might be needed to access the interior of the camper van. Beyond the fire truck, he could see that the helicopter had landed and the crew were getting out and loading the equipment they needed onto a stretcher. At that distance, with their flight suits and helmets on, it was impossible to recognise anyone but...there was a smaller figure amongst them who seemed to be working with a determination and focus that sent a chill down Cade's spine.

He shook it off. No… It *couldn't* be…

By the time he'd rapidly relayed what information he had about the number of victims in the camper van, where they were and what condition they were in as far as he could tell, the helicopter crew had covered the distance between their landing point and when Cade turned his head again they were more than close enough to recognise someone he knew. Like Tom. And the woman walking beside him.

That chill that he'd felt moments ago was still there but it was becoming something very different as it spread. By the time he'd pulled in a breath it was a heat filling his chest that was a powerful mix of utter disbelief and…and *anger*…

Fury, even.

His eyes were narrowing as he took a step closer to Joanna Bishop. He lowered his voice, instinctively keeping what he was saying between only the two of them, but it had the effect of making his words even more vehement.

'What the *hell* do you think *you're* doing here?'

CHAPTER TWELVE

THIS WAS A moment like no other.

Jo had never experienced a 'sliding doors' kind of moment when it was easy to recognise a decision that had changed the whole course of her life, but this was how she'd met Cade Cameron, wasn't it? She'd climbed out of a helicopter and walked into his life and, by the time they'd worked together in that tense situation when it seemed likely that they'd have to amputate a young woman's leg in order to save her life, she had known that this meeting was significant.

The flashback was instantaneous and took only a heartbeat of time. Jo could hear the engine noise of the helicopter diminishing behind her as it was shut down. She could hear the pneumatic gear from the fire service being set up and tested and the shouts of officers as they worked on getting the unstable vehicle safe to approach. She could see a pile of damaged bicycles and paramedics working with at least half a dozen people who were sitting or lying on blankets that had been laid on the ground.

That was where she needed to be and where she would be in a matter of seconds. What felt like an unfair attack from Cade wasn't about to slow her down but, even as she kept walking, Jo was momentarily caught by that flashback. And she must have slowed a little because Tom was well ahead of her within a few steps. Or had Tom heard the outrage in Cade's voice and sped up to avoid being caught in what was clearly a very personal exchange?

What felt like the opening salvo of a confrontation was the jarring note in what was almost a recreation of the first time they'd met, with Jo stepping out of a helicopter to walk into Cade's professional arena. It wouldn't be happening at all if she'd made a different choice the day they'd met and had gone through a different set of doors. She'd known that an invitation from Cade had been hanging there that day, just waiting for her to decide whether or not she wanted to accept it. She'd seen the admiration in his eyes. She'd known perfectly well that he was interested in more than an update on their patient when he'd written his phone number on her glove.

But this…this couldn't be more different. There was nothing like admiration in his eyes right now. Cade was so *angry* with her. It looked as if she was the last person he wanted to see. That she couldn't possibly do anything that could earn his approval, let alone his admiration. If he'd looked remotely like that the first time they'd met she would never have sent that text message to accept that invitation. They would never have got to 'know each other' so well, with all the emotional, and now physical, repercussions.

There were echoes there of the way Jo's parents had looked at her all too often as she'd been growing up. Her father annoyed that he was being disturbed, with any approval or affection so closely guarded it was almost impossible to get within touching distance. Her mother disappointed, yet again, because she wasn't behaving in an acceptable manner.

There was another layer over that too, with a flash of remembering the way Cade had pushed her away when they'd worked together at the scene of that horrific car crash when they'd had to fight to save the life of that young boy. Another sliding doors moment, perhaps, because she'd been quite prepared to walk away from any kind of relationship with Cade at that point? Until she'd learned that there was a very good reason why he'd been so upset.

And suddenly Jo knew exactly why he was reacting like this now. Because she was pregnant. With his child. It wasn't that he cared that she might be putting herself in danger, was it? It was because there was something—some*one*—far more important at stake.

And, just as suddenly, Cade wasn't the only person who was angry because maybe that was Jo's only defence against having her heart broken that little bit more. Did he really think that she was about to put this precious baby she was carrying into danger? She was trusting him by letting him close enough to be the father he wanted to be to this child, but where was *his* trust? It made no difference that she'd known it would be wise to step back from this part of her job because of her pregnancy. Or maybe it did. Maybe she was feeling guilty that she'd followed her instincts of needing to help and she was angry with herself as well as Cade. Or maybe she was automatically tapping into the mode where she'd always had to fight for the things she wanted, or needed, for herself even when she knew she was losing the battle. When she simply wasn't good enough…

Whatever…

'I'm doing exactly the same thing here that you are, I expect,' she snapped. 'My *job*…'

Cade was still right beside Jo as she reached the treatment area for the cyclists, where Tom was standing in front of a whiteboard that was keeping track of patients, their status and their injuries, talking to a fire officer who was wearing a vest designating him as the scene commander. Cade stooped to pick up a paramedic kit from where equipment and supplies were being stored and then turned away to head to the edge of road where she could see the cluster of rescue personnel focused on what was happening below them.

'Stay here,' Cade ordered Jo. 'Do *not*, under any circumstances, come anywhere near where we're working on the camper van.'

He still looked furious as he slung the strap of the pack over one shoulder and strode away but Jo could feel her own anger dissipating into a fleeting acknowledgement of something else. Sadness that she was being ordered around like someone who'd failed to do what was expected of her? Or perhaps it was a poignancy that her baby had something she would never have herself, a person who loved her enough to do whatever it took to protect her?

Again, whatever…

This wasn't the time to unpick any stray emotions. As she'd told Cade, Jo was here to do her job and that was the only thing she was going to focus on. There would, undoubtedly, be way too much time to think about any personal issues later.

The anger wouldn't go away.

Cade might have been able to shut down any personal considerations the moment he'd climbed back down the slope to where steel cables were now preventing the van from sliding or even rolling any further, but that knot of emotion was still there in his gut and it wasn't acceptable.

He had a job to do here and he couldn't allow a distraction that might interfere with his focus on the first patient. The driver of the van had regained consciousness by the time he got close enough to assess him thoroughly but his confusion and combativeness suggested that he had a significant head injury and it would make the task of extricating him a danger to everybody involved, including the patient. It wasn't going to be possible to get to his wife or the children in the back until he was out and that added to the urgency.

It should have made it easy to completely forget the shock of seeing Jo on scene, but that knot in his stomach wouldn't go away. It wasn't interfering as Cade sorted his assessment and treatment priorities but he could feel it as a background niggle that he knew he'd have to deal with later.

In the meantime, sedation was needed, which meant IV access was a priority. A C collar was called for because the mechanism of injury could well have caused cervical spine trauma. Oxygen was on this list and further interventions to secure the man's airway could well be necessary. An extrication device that fitted like a vest and immobilised the spine, neck and head would have to be used to lift the patient from the vehicle. A baseline set of vital signs would let him know what the most urgent action was going to be. Cade tried to catch a flailing arm and wrist to check both the heart rate and rhythm and get at least a rough gauge of blood pressure as he watched and listened to assess respiratory effort.

'Take it easy, mate. I'm just trying to help. Try not to move just yet.'

Jules was trying to calm her husband from where she was still trapped in the passenger seat. 'Stay still, Pete. It's okay…we're going to be okay…'

Pete's knuckles narrowly missed Cade's chin. 'I need another medic down here,' he told the nearest fire officer. 'Stat.'

'Sure thing. Want us to bring the doctor down as well?'

'*No*…' Cade's response was emphatic. 'Dr Bishop is not to come down here. Send another HEMS crew member, please.'

Okay…so maybe that niggle wasn't quite far enough in the background but, good grief…how could she be taking a risk like this? Even being a passenger in a helicopter was bad enough. Surely Jo, of all people, knew how fragile life could be. For anyone, but especially for vulnerable children or an unborn baby…

It was Tom who joined him to work in the cramped and difficult space that the front seat of the van provided. The look he flicked Cade made him wonder if something had been said about Jo not being allowed to work down here with him but Tom made no comment. He was already completely focused on what was clearly going to be a challenging job ahead of them.

Accident scenes that involved a lot of emergency services personnel were a bit like a nightmare version of an emergency department for Jo. They were centred around the same injuries and sometimes medical events that she was well used to dealing with in a hospital setting but the environment and resources were far more chaotic out in the field and you couldn't summon backup or push a cardiac arrest button knowing that more staff and equipment would arrive in seconds.

It was the reason Jo had always loved this part of her job, but today it seemed noisier and more challenging than it ever had before. Stressful, that was the word for it. It didn't help that there was still no sign of what was likely to be the most seriously injured patient in this incident being extricated from his vehicle so he could be stabilised and taken to that nicely controlled emergency department that was waiting for him.

'What's happening down the bank?' she asked the scene commander as he stepped

back to let two ambulance officers steer a
stretcher towards a waiting ambulance.

'They're still working on getting the guy
out. Shouldn't be too much longer. How's it
going here?'

'Under control. We've pretty much sorted
all the cyclists. That patient going now has
a probable fracture/dislocation of his ankle.
The others have some cuts and bruises but
they're all okay to transport themselves and
they want to stay here and sort out the bikes.'

'What about that woman with the neck
injury?'

'She was the first to go by ambulance—
about ten minutes ago. I don't think it was
a serious injury. The tingling in her hands
disappeared as soon as she stopped hyper-
ventilating but she'll get properly checked
out at hospital.'

Jo wanted to go and look over the edge
of the road to see what was happening but
she could still hear Cade ordering her not
to go near that part of the scene under any
circumstances. Being so busy with the injured cyclists had meant she hadn't had an
opportunity to think about how angry he'd
been that she was here but there was nothing to distract her now. Except that she was
also aware of something else that was adding

to her stress levels. As usual with a HEMS callout, she hadn't taken the time to go to the bathroom before rushing up to the roof-top helipad but it wasn't usually a problem because the adrenaline that came with this kind of work could shut down the need for as long as an emergency took.

She'd never had a baby pressing on her bladder before, though, had she?

Cade's baby.

Her own anger had long since evaporated. Right now she had the kind of squeeze on her heart that she'd had when she'd first heard Cade's tragic story. The kind of squeeze that had only become more painful the more she'd fallen in love with him. He was just trying to protect himself, wasn't he? And if it was so hard he had to use anger as a shield now, would he even be able to keep those barriers in place at all when he was able to hold his baby in his own arms?

'You think it'll be a few minutes before they bring up the driver?'

'Yep. They were just starting to get him into that jacket thing they use. He'll have to be secured to the scoop stretcher and then brought up the bank. We'll be able to get to the woman and children then, so it'll get busy again.'

'I'm going up the road for a minute or so,' Jo told him. 'Nature's calling.'

The scene commander gave her a thumbs-up sign. 'No worries. Don't go far away, will you? You might be needed soon.'

'I won't.'

Jo had no intention of going any further than she needed to in order to find a private spot. There was plenty of vegetation and large rocks on the slope between the road and the river and it wasn't so steep further up the road towards where the helicopter had landed. There was nothing else she needed to do at the moment and she'd be back in plenty of time to help Tom and the other paramedics still on scene to treat and load the van driver.

She took extra care to watch her footing so that she didn't slip as she climbed a short distance down from the edge of the road and then searched for a sheltered space behind rocks or a bush. If she couldn't see anyone else, they wouldn't be able to see her, would they? A minute or two later, she was zipping up her flight suit again, feeling much less stressed, and she closed her eyes to let out a long breath.

That was when she heard it.

An odd noise.

It sounded like…what…a lamb bleating? It made Jo take a few more steps down the slope, anyway, to see what it was and she found herself much closer to the river. And, yes…it did look like a lamb. A small, white shape near the water's edge. Except… Jo took another step, trying to focus. Trying to make sense of the movement she could see. It wasn't a lamb, she realised. It was a very small child, wearing just a nappy and a white singlet. Her head swerving, Jo realised she could see the back of the camper van now that she was away from the shelter of the bushes and rocks. She could see the smashed window in the van's back door. Was that where the baby had come from? Why had nobody noticed? Would they hear her if she shouted loudly enough?

Another blink to check on the child and she found it was standing up. Wobbling on small, chubby legs. Heading straight for the edge of the river. It was less than twenty metres away from where Jo was, but it was too far. And anyone near the van who heard her shouting would be even further away. The river might not be huge but she could see that there was a decent current. More than enough to snatch a baby and wash it away.

There was a much steeper slope before

the ground levelled off near the river but Jo couldn't take the time to search for a safer route. She did her best to avoid injuring herself by sitting down on her bottom and pushing herself into a slide so that she didn't fall. She held her breath as she started moving and sent up a silent plea that she would get there in time.

The twist in the tail of this rescue mission was completely unexpected.

Every pair of hands that could get close enough to the camper van had been utilised to get access to the injured driver and get him out safely. Cocooned in a cervical collar, the extrication device that wrapped around his body and warm blankets beneath the straps of a basket stretcher, he was being passed from handhold to handhold by the rescue workers positioned on the steep slope between the van and the road where the helicopter was waiting to transport him to hospital.

The most difficult aspect of this rescue had been successfully completed as far as Cade and the others were aware. Tom was heading up with the stretcher. He and the rest of his HEMS crew could take over. Cade was now focused on getting Jules and her children out. The young mother did have a fractured wrist, which Cade swiftly splinted. He couldn't tell if her ankle was broken or only sprained, but her foot wasn't badly trapped after all and he'd been able to ease it out of her shoe to get her free. She refused to climb out of the van before her children, however, reaching through the gap between the front seats.

'Hayley? Come here, darling. It's okay… we're going to get out now.'

The young girl squeezed through the gap and Cade lifted her out to pass her into the arms of a waiting fire officer.

'Does anything hurt, sweetheart?' he asked.

She shook her head but burst into tears. 'I want Mummy…'

'I'm coming,' Jules called. 'Jamie? Where's Danny?'

'He's asleep. Under the duvet.'

'How old is Danny?' Cade was leaning into the van, one knee on the driver's seat.

'Fifteen months. He's our baby.' Jules was twisting her body, trying to see into the back. 'Can you get in through the back door?'

'There's a tree blocking it.' Did he need to get the firies to use their cutting gear on the rear of the van? They were talking about a baby here. A silent baby.

'Where is he, Jamie?' There was an edge of panic in Jules' voice. 'I can't see.'

Cade could see into the back. He could see Jamie sitting in the nest of crumpled bedding. He could see the duvet covered lump beside the small boy that had to be the sleeping baby, but something didn't feel right. Cade could actually feel the hairs on the back of his neck rising as he put his arms through the gap and pulled at a corner of the duvet he could reach. One good tug and he uncovered the lump.

'Oh, my God,' Jules said. 'That's a pillow... Where's *Danny*?'

Cade's gaze flicked up to the smashed window in the back door. Had the baby been thrown clear? Was he lying badly injured and hidden in the undergrowth? He was out of the van before he'd taken his next breath. Behind it as he instructed the rest of the team to get Jules and Jamie out. He could see more now. All the way down to the river, which wasn't that far away. His gaze snagged on a white blob at the water's edge but then swerved sideways. The bright orange of a flight suit was far more eye-catching.

He knew who it was, of course. And he knew he was seeing the moment just after Jo must have fallen because he could see the speed with which her body was moving—straight towards the rocks that bordered the river.

'*No...*'

Maybe a cloud happened to block the sun at precisely that point in time. Or maybe he had just imagined it, but Cade was always going to remember the way the entire world seemed to have dimmed as he began to run.

It wasn't the first time Jo had been thankful for the steel-capped boots she always wore with her flight suit for a HEMS callout. She used her foot to slow and then break her slide well before she reached the bottom of the slope. She was on her feet a heartbeat later and had the baby in her arms before she'd even pulled in a new breath.

Almost in the same moment, she found she was herself in someone's arms.

But it wasn't simply someone. It was Cade. There were others right behind him. People who took a baby who seemed miraculously unharmed, leaving Cade to help Jo back up to the road.

Except he didn't move straight away. Instead, Jo could feel the grip of his arms tighten around her.

'Are you sure you're okay? I saw you fall…'

'I'm fine.' Although Jo could feel that she was trembling. 'I wasn't falling, I was sliding. I *had* to, Cade… I had to get to the baby before he went into the river.'

'I know…'

'I'm sorry…'

'What for?'

'Being here. I *could* have fallen.' Jo could feel tears rolling down her face as the fright kicked in. She'd done something that could have been catastrophic. Her next words were no more than a whisper. 'I could have hurt our baby.'

Cade's baby. She could have repeated a history that would have destroyed this man she loved so much. It would have destroyed her. Cade had every right to be even more angry with her than he had been when he'd seen her arrive. But he didn't seem angry as he cradled her body in his arms. He certainly didn't sound angry when he spoke, his lips close to her ear.

'I could have lost *you*…and, right now, that's all I can think about.'

Jo blinked. That didn't make sense. The baby was more important than anything else. It was the only reason Cade intended to stay in her life, wasn't it? The only reason he'd asked her to marry him?

'I was wrong.' Cade's voice was a low growl that seemed to be answering a question Jo hadn't asked aloud. 'I guess it's true that you don't know what you've got till it's gone, and when I saw you falling I knew…'

Good grief…it sounded as if Cade's words were being choked by tears.

'I knew what it would be like if you *were* gone and…and it felt like it would be the end of the world. I love you, Jo.' There was amazement in his voice. 'I didn't think I could ever feel that again but… I do. I love you. I think I always have.'

Yeah…that heartbreaking catch in his voice conveyed a depth of emotion that was utterly compelling. The kind of emotion that stole your breath and squeezed your heart so hard it hurt. The kind Jo had been feeling herself ever since she'd fallen in love with Cade.

'Me too,' was all that she could whisper.

Cade's radio crackled into life and almost

drowned her words but she knew that she'd been heard. She could see it in his eyes.

'You guys okay down there? Need any help?'

Cade cleared his throat and pushed the button to respond. 'We're on our way. We're all good.'

He caught Jo's gaze and, for the first time in weeks, they had one of those silent conversations that could happen in a heartbeat.

Are we good?

Yes... So good...

We can't talk now.

No. We've got a job to finish.

We'll talk later, though.

Oh, we absolutely will.

They began the scramble back to road level, with Cade keeping a tight hold on Jo's hand. He didn't catch her gaze again until they were about to step back into their professional roles. Tom was already in the helicopter with their patient and the rotors were picking up speed. Geoff and another ambulance crew were caring for the rest of the rescued family, who would be able to be transported by road. It was time to put the finishing touches on this mission.

So it was merely another blink of an eye

that they shared. Just a graze of eye contact, but it was more than enough for Jo.

I do love you. Cade looked as stunned by the revelation as she was feeling. *More than I could ever tell you.*

You just did, Cade. Jo could feel her lips tilting into a misty smile. *You just did.*

EPILOGUE

A month later...

HE WAS THE luckiest man on earth.

He was being given, quite literally, a new life. On more than one level.

The ability to feel love was an unexpected gift. And yes, that came with risk and he still had moments when fear could edge its way in, but it was worth it because, without taking that risk, you could never feel like this. Like you had found the very best of what life could offer. That simply living each day was so much more meaningful and that your future was so much more exciting because you had someone to share it with.

If you were really lucky, the person you loved felt the same way about you, and if you were as lucky as Cade Cameron that person was an extraordinary woman who had admitted that she had so much love to give. Love that she'd bottled up because she'd never had someone who loved her back. But now she did and she was choosing to give all that love to *him*. And their child, of course, but for now it was mostly just for him and he was going to make the most of every minute.

Would he be pushing his luck if he asked the question that was, once again, burning a hole in his brain? It had been pushed aside in the last weeks because life had got so busy, what with work and going public with their relationship and Jo's pregnancy. With moving in together and house hunting and antenatal appointments. And with using every possible free moment to just be together and get used to this miracle of loving and being loved. He couldn't ask for any more than that, anyway. Could he?

'There you go…' It might be too dark to see the smile on Jo's face but he could hear it in her voice. 'I knew she'd wake up as soon as I started to go to sleep. Did you feel that?'

Of course he had. Cade had his hand resting gently on the increasingly rounded bump of Jo's belly, his fingers splayed, and he'd felt the ripple of movement beneath them as a sensation that had been picked up by every cell in his own body.

'Hey, Bump…' He stroked Jo's skin, knowing that the baby must be able to feel his touch. 'How're you doing in there?'

Jo laid her hand on top of his and kept it there as the baby moved again. A distinct kick, this time.

'I've got an idea.' Cade grinned. 'Kick once for "yes" and don't kick for "no", okay?'

Jo laughed. 'Yeah…right… Good luck with that.'

Cade wasn't deterred. 'What did you think of the house we looked at today, Bump? The one with the view of the harbour and that big garden with the swing. Did you like it? Do you think we should buy it?'

They both felt the contact of the baby's foot against their hands.

'I guess that's settled.' Cade grinned. He leaned sideways to kiss Jo. 'Unless you disagree?'

'It *was* a lovely house.' Jo was smiling again. 'A real family home.'

There was a note in her voice that made him kiss her again. 'That's what we need. Because we're going to be a *real* family.'

'Mmm…'

'If we bought it now, we could be all

moved in and settled in a couple of months, well before Bump's birthday.'

'As long as we didn't make the settlement date for when you're in Europe. You'll be away for a week for that conference. Have you booked your tickets yet?'

'I was going to talk to you about that.' Cade was smiling. 'I was hoping you might like to come with me. You've never been to Prague, have you?'

'No. But I had Hanna telling me that it was on the top of her bucket list today. She's hoping to go to that conference herself. She reckoned she could kill two birds with one stone—some professional development plus an adventure.'

'Adventures are good.' Cade still had his hand on Jo's belly, although it felt as if Bump had gone back to sleep. 'We're good at adventures. You should come.'

'But... I wouldn't be allowed to fly by then, would I?'

'You can fly up to thirty-six weeks, if there are no complications. There's plenty of time.'

Jo had woven her fingers through Cade's. 'It could be our first family holiday. Sort of.'

Cade took a deep breath. 'It could be our honeymoon.'

He held his breath in the silence that followed his words.

'Are you…are you asking me to marry you?'

'Yes. But not because we're having a baby together. Because I love you. The way you always have and always will deserve to be loved.' He pressed his lips against Jo's hair. 'The way I will love you as long as I have breath in my body.' He had to clear the sudden lump in his throat. 'Will you? Will you marry me?'

Jo sounded as if she had a lump in her own throat. 'I was really hoping you'd ask me again,' she said softly. 'Ever since what was probably the last helicopter mission I'll ever go on. When I knew that you loved me as much as I love you.'

'Is that a "yes"?'

Jo was smiling through tears now. '*Yes…*'

The kick against their hands surprised them both into laughter and Cade had to blink back his own tears.

'I guess that makes it unanimous.'

Yep…there was no doubt about it.

He was the luckiest man on earth.

* * * * *